Neptune's Garden
& Other Adventures

By
Ron Chandler

Copyright 2017 Ron Chandler
All rights reserved.

This is a work of fiction. Names, characters, businesses, places, events and incidents are either the products of the author's imagination or used in a fictitious manner. Any resemblance to actual persons, living or dead, or actual events is purely coincidental.

The cover was illustrated and designed by Cait May, whose work is a product of her imagination and ingenuity.

Edited by Mia R. Cortez

Book layout by www.ebooklaunch.com

Contents

Fashionably Late 1
The Omen 7
Don't Tread On Me 17
The Storm 33
Kerry and the Keys 43
Dust 59
Neptune's Garden 71
Ceremonious Cicadas 101
Bear of the Bog 103
A Hero for Herons 113
Red Cloud 127
Mission Control to Thomas Hardy 141

Fashionably Late

KENNETH'S MOTHER TAUGHT HIM to always be fashionably late. He was late when he met his girlfriend, Sharon, at Ram's Head Tavern on Thursday night, showing up after Puddle of Mudd had already taken the stage. He found her by text in that darkened venue with a cell phone that had a screen as bright as a lighthouse beacon. And he was two innings late when he went to see the Orioles at Camden Yards the weekend before, missing the home run blast by Adam Jones that landed in the left field seats. So he figured the same should be true of his new hobby: hiking. He went to Champion Sporting Goods the day of the event and texted the following message to the guy in charge:

Stopped 2 buy XLNT gear 4 hike 2day. Will B a few minutes L8. PLZ W8. THX.

The hike leader, Bill, wasn't even fazed. He had scheduled the Sugarloaf Mountain hike to begin at 5:30 p.m. to beat the heat of an August Sunday. This guy, Kenneth, was just another 404 going on his first hike. He was sure his group could w8 an extra 15 minutes so he typed back:

CU whenever.

When Kenneth got there about a dozen hikers, looking casual in jeans and a rainbow of blouses and T-shirts, were waiting in the parking lot ready to go, but they had to wait a bit longer as he lathered sun-block on his skin and laced up his new hiking boots with the 1-inch sole. He unfurled a slick rain jacket and flipped it inside out to show everyone how it could be converted to a regular jacket.

The burly hike leader wasn't impressed. He simply gazed at the sky and asked, "Are there any clouds up there?"

Kenneth looked up and didn't see one speck of cumulous or cirrus clouds.

The hike leader chuckled and said, "Put that back in your car."

Kenneth returned to his car and tossed the jacket in the trunk, but he was sure he had all the other gear he needed for the hike.

"Let's go!" barked Bill.

The hikers swung their knapsacks onto their backs and fell into line, eager to begin their trek.

Bill led them up a winding trail, full of rocks and stone ledges, to the top of Sugarloaf Mountain. Everyone gathered at an overlook. Down below, the tangerine sunlight was melting into the Potomac River valley. While some hikers took photos and others gawked at the view, Kenneth chomped on an energy bar made from granola and then tore open his other snacks - a Harvest Power Bar made from whole grain, fruit and chunks of chocolate, a Honey-Stinger made from honey, ginseng and kola nut and other bars called Caramel Crisp and Blueberry Burst. He licked his lips after each bite while the other hikers drooled.

"Thanks, Slim," remarked one middle-aged woman. "I'm trying to lose weight and you're waving those things in front of my face."

"I can let you have a Honey-Stinger for two dollars."

The woman stomped away, muttering something nasty about men.

Bill called out, "Let's go!" and led them down the other side of the mountain into the woods. They tread on a trail along a stream and hiked on another along a ridge. They saw a stone cairn marking a footpath to a second overlook, White Rocks. They followed that path in and out of ravines and climbed a mound of rocks. Sitting there gulping water, they watched the sun turn crimson on the horizon, but a pale light still glowed in the sky above them.

Kenneth took out his camera, snapped on a wide-angle lens, and moved about the rocks clicking photos of the sunset.

"What are you doing?" asked the hike leader. "We got to get out of here before the sunlight disappears."

The rest of the hikers were lined up with their knapsacks slung onto their backs, taking one last sip of water.

"Hey, Bill, I need a couple more minutes," said Kenneth.

"We got to get moving."

"You're jealous because I own a Nikon 550 and you don't."

"I don't care about your camera," said the hike leader. "We got two more miles to go and only a half hour of daylight left."

"I got all the gear I need in my knapsack," bragged Kenneth. He squatted down to snap another photo. "I'm going to post these pictures on my Facebook page and show everybody how cool I am."

"We can't wait for you," said Bill.

"You're not waiting for him?" asked another hiker with a worried look.

The middle-aged woman quipped, "Maybe Slim is too cool to hike with us."

"Let's go!' barked Bill.

The group set off through the woods on the trail back to the parking lot, leaving him behind. Kenneth took 14 more photos that would *wow!* everybody. He zipped up the camera in his knapsack and resumed the hike, but the sunlight had faded and now a luminous fog was rising up from the damp ground and his feet were cloaked in darkness. He took off running down the trail, hoping he could do the whole two miles in 15 minutes, but he was going up and down knolls and had to stop to find the trail markers on the trees and before he realized it…there was no light at all. He could barely see as he rummaged through his knapsack for a flashlight.

"No…Don't tell me…" he screamed to himself. "I forgot to buy a flashlight. How stupid am I?"

He felt his heart pounding in his chest and heard his breathing become as rapid as the panting of a dog.

"My cell phone!"

Yes! That's was it. He could dial 911 and get help. But when he pulled out his cell phone and dialed the number, nothing happened. The phone was useless because there was no cell tower nearby to carry the signal. He was stuck on a mountainside in the middle of nowhere.

"What am I going to do?" he mumbled to himself. "The light!"

The screen of the cell phone was projecting enough light so he could see the dirt trail before him. He held it forward and splashed through a puddle near a trickling stream, over another little knoll, down into a ravine, and along another stream. He climbed a ridge and saw the lights of a house, far off in the valley, shining like the stars of a constellation. Perhaps he could connect to a cell phone tower and to civilization. He typed a text message to a friend:

L (Larry), need Ur help. Lost in woods on Sugarloaf. K.

Kenneth waited for what seemed like an eternity. He heard the last trilling and chirping of the birds as they settled down in the treetops, a squirrel's claws scratching bark as it raced around a trunk, and the buzz of a bee heading back to the hive. A message appeared on the screen:

WGRUP? (What game are you playing?)

To which he typed:

RL (Real life)

To which Larry replied:

K, that's a bumR. Will trace GPS from P (phone) 4 resQ squad. L.

Just then the screen flickered and Kenneth thought about all the phone calls he had made and text messages he had sent in the past two days since the battery was recharged and right before the screen went black he typed in:

OMG (Oh my God!)

Kenneth looked up into the pitch-black sky and couldn't see one star or moonbeam to show him the way out of the woods. He felt a chill because the sun had gone down and the heat no longer radiated from the ground.

"Damn it," he screamed. "Why did I leave my jacket in the car?"

Cicadas rasped from a nearby tree.

"Oh, God," pleaded Kenneth. "If there is a God, please help me."

But no help came.

He staggered about, bumping into trees, impaling himself on a thorny bush, and twisting his ankle when his leg fell into a hole. It became colder and colder as the temperature plunged from the high 80s to the low 50s. He cleared a space in the brush by taking a broken branch and raking the decayed leaves, left over from last autumn, up on one side. Sitting on the ground, he scooped the leaves on top his legs and stomach to keep warm. He turned over and laid face down in the dirt, covering his head with his arms. The cicadas were roaring, the crickets seemed to be beating on pots and pans, and the sound of an animal screaming came from somewhere deep in the woods, making him shudder. He burrowed deeper into Mother Earth and laid there as motionless as a log. He lapsed in and out of sleep all night and then…

A thrush twittered in a nearby bush and twilight twinkled between the trees. More birdsong sprung up throughout the woods until it was as loud as a symphony. Even though it was daybreak, it felt damp and cold. Kenneth got up. Something dangled from his ear. "Ew!" He brushed his hair and spun around in a panic because purplish-black caterpillars were hanging all over him. He dashed up a hill and twirled around again and again like the devil doing a mad dance, throwing off the creepy crawlers.

Kenneth hustled back and slung on his knapsack, which was wet with mud. He bushwhacked through the woods toward the sunrise, but after going only 20 yards he came upon a road going upwards. *JMT (Just my luck)*, he thought, *I'm SSIF (So stupid it's funny)*. He hiked along the road toward the parking lot near the top of the mountain.

He trudged upward with twigs stuck in his hair, clothes coated with mud, leaves and crushed caterpillars clinging to his pants. His knapsack stuck out like a deformed hump, making him look like a crustacean that had just crawled out of the muck of the Chesapeake Bay. A couple joggers went by and snickered.

Through a gap in the trees he saw his Toyota in the parking lot, grateful it was still there and he was in one piece. He raced across the asphalt and flung his knapsack in the backseat and plopped in the front. When he turned on the motor, the digital clock in the dashboard read: 8:45 a.m. He had to be at work at nine. He would have to drive home, take a shower, grab something from the refrig to eat, get dressed, and drive to work. But first he would call from a landline and tell his boss that he would be fashionably L8.

The Omen

MIKE HEARD WATER DRIPPING off their paddles as the canoe sliced through the Okefenokee Swamp. Out in the open water, which reflected the blue sky, he smelled the white lilies blooming in the morning sun and the scent of pine sap carried by a mild breeze. Yellow warblers flitted in-between bushes and danced in midair to the sound of their song, which was a sweet luting. He saw his sister, Claire, pointing to a summer tanager, its rose-red plumage standing out in a stunted oak. It sung, *pik-i-tuk-i-tuk*. The canoe glided underneath the forest canopy. The odor turned putrid with the decay of fallen leaves and tannic acid percolating from tree roots, coloring the swamp black. Foggy mist wafted a few feet high and dispersed. Mike felt drops of moisture and realized that everything inside the canoe was becoming wet. When they slid by a submerged log, he kept a careful lookout for alligators. The canoe came near a giant cypress, its knobby knees poking out of the blackness.

"I see one," hissed his brother, Gilbert.

Mike heard an eerie song from above, *hoo…hoo-oo…hoo…hoo*, the notes shifting tone from high to low to high. He spotted a great-horned owl perched on a sycamore branch gobbling down a squirrel, crunching its bones and furry pelt. He scanned the waterline and surrounding foliage for anything dangerous, then urged, "Go for it."

Gilbert stepped into the knee-deep water with his stocky frame hunched forward like a football linebacker waiting for the next play. This one had to be larger than the last one they caught. Mike wondered whether its slithery body was wrapped around a tree trunk or submerged beneath the mud like a Chinese New Year's dragon. Either way his brother held the tongs over the surface of the swamp, ready for anything.

Mike watched his brother, whose block face tightened with concern, making it appear leaner. The last python they caught gave them a struggle. Even though they placed the snake in a cloth bag, it squirmed around in the canoe bottom, shifting its shape. It flipped to the right side of the gunwale, and everybody had to lean left to keep the canoe from tipping over. When they got to the ranger station, it stayed coiled in the bag. Gilbert used tongs to grip the python's head and pull it out, its tail slithering on the ground like a garden hose squirting water everywhere. They grabbed and straightened out the snake for the ranger to measure its length: 12 feet. The ranger paid them $300 for the specimen because it was *an invasive species disrupting the ecological balance of the wetland*. The money would pay for Gilbert's spring semester in college. Still it wasn't enough. They had plenty more work left to do. Mike knew this one was bigger by the way his brother acted. He heard the air singing. In that split second the colors of the marsh became clearer, the scents more intoxicating, and the humidity settled on his skin with a light touch. He tilted his chin up in anticipation.

"Argh!" Gilbert tottered backwards. "What the…" An arrow pierced his shoulder with blood on the part of the shaft that had gone through.

"Huh?" gasped Mike.

"What happened?" asked Claire.

"Some jerk shot him," yelled Mike. "We got to help him."

They paddled over there and grabbed their brother, whose body wobbled. They helped him clamber into the canoe.

"I can't believe this," said Gilbert, looking at the feathered shaft sticking out in front of him. Then he screamed loud enough for anyone who was out there to hear him, "I will get you, bastard."

Mike scanned the distant trees with his binoculars, searching for the archer. He spotted him. Standing high on a cypress branch was a tall, thin man with the face of a ghoul, streaks of black paint forming a demonic mask.

"Pull it out," demanded Gilbert.

"Don't," warned Claire, whose high-pitched voice was shrill with worry. "The wound will hemorrhage."

"Sit down," said Mike.

Gilbert plopped down in the middle of the canoe, dazed and clutching his shoulder. Mike and Claire paddled ferociously back to their put-in point, but the sound of their paddles slapping the water couldn't drown out their brother's moans. Claire kept dialing 911, but no cell towers were out in the swamp to carry the signal. When they got to the canal, a call went through. She arranged for an ambulance to meet them on the way back to town. They pulled their canoe ashore and tossed the paddles aside. They carried him to their SUV and raced down a dirt lane by the canal. Blood dripped down Gilbert's shirt as he slumped in the backseat. When they got to the crossroad, the ambulance was waiting.

The paramedics laid Gilbert on a stretcher on his side, the arrow still lodged in his shoulder. They injected him with morphine to deaden the pain and loaded the stretcher in the ambulance. The siren wailed as the ambulance took off.

By the time they got him to the hospital, Gilbert's head was filled with visions and made him speak in delirium. The paramedics wheeled him into the emergency room where a team of doctors and nurses pounced on him. One sawed off the back of the arrow. Another pulled the remaining shaft out through the front of his shoulder. Blood squirted everywhere. Nurses pressed down on the wounds to slow the bleeding while the first doctor sutured the tissue. "A negative," someone said. A nurse hooked a pint bag of blood to a stand and switched on the IV drip. Gilbert lapsed into unconsciousness as the transfusion flowed into him. Over a hundred stitches were needed to close the gaping holes in his body. The second doctor bandaged the wounds by wrapping gauze around his torso.

Two days later, Gilbert came to. He was no longer on an IV drip and could eat solid food. A nurse came into the room and announced, "Sheriff Barnes would like to chat with you."

A stocky man in a light blue shirt highlighted by a silver badge and gray pants plodded into the room. He had a thick sunburned neck, mottled face, gray hair swept to one side, and heavy-lidded eyes. He carried the two parts of the arrow in a clear plastic evidence bag. He spoke in a thoughtful tone, "I had my deputy take a look at this item - the shaft (which had a color like orange pekoe tea), the flint tip (sharpened to a hard marbled-white point), and the feathers at the end (similar to the black plume of a vulture). He tells me, *It is Choctaw!*"

"Choctaw Indians," gasped Mike.

Gilbert sat up in bed and screamed, "We should have killed them all."

"Not so fast," said Sheriff Barnes. "The Choctaws originally lived in Alabama and Mississippi. Now they reside on a reservation in Oklahoma. This is a bit east of their range. The Seminoles used to come this far north a long time ago. I reckon it may have been carved by a hunter around here. If that is so, his shot may have gone wide. There are plenty of deer and game birds out there on the marsh."

"He almost killed me!" shouted Gilbert. "Do something."

"I'll go out there tomorrow and take a look around."

"I'll go with you," huffed Mike. "That's my brother lying there. I can show you where we were."

"Please yourself," stated the sheriff. "It'll probably make no difference."

The next day Mike boarded the sheriff's fan boat at the town dock. When Sheriff Barnes turned on the motor, the whirling blade made the bow lift up. They planed across the water into the canal's channel. Instead of going into the swampy forest where he and his sister were earlier in the week, the sheriff guided the fan boat along the canal, occasionally stopping to inspect bait lines. A three-foot gator thrashed about in the water hooked to one line. Another had snared a six-foot long python that slithered nearby in the grass. Then Sheriff Barnes came to a worn-out dock and brought the fan boat alongside. They clambered onto the planks.

"Who's that on our dock?" asked a grandfatherly-looking man peering through the top of bifocals. He had leathery skin and sunken eyes.

"Hey, boy," called out another man with big arms who wore hip-waders and a fishing vest with a dozen pockets. "You should be skedaddling in a dance hall with those heavy boots." He turned to another fellow who was barefoot and asked, "Garth, what do you think of those there boots?"

The barefoot man, who wore cutoff jeans and whose beard was flecked with gray, drawled, "I ain't wore shoes since I can remember."

Sheriff Barnes said, "This boy, Mike, is from Virginia."

"Ginny boots stomping on our dock?" laughed the elderly man.

"His brother got shot with an arrow," stated the sheriff, "…Choctaw."

"Choctaw?" asked the man with big arms.

Nobody said anything for a spell. Cicadas rasped from a nearby tree and a covey of sparrows foraged for seeds in the grass, chirping a melody. The water in the canal washed against the dock.

"I'm thinking you might take him on," said Sheriff Barnes. "Give him a cut."

"Ten percent is all he's worth," said the elderly man.

"They'll teach you well," stated Sheriff Barnes.

"I know what I'm doing," huffed Mike.

"You wear those boots and you know what you're doing?" asked the big-armed man.

The other guys snickered.

Mike was fond of his heavy hiking boots, which reminded him of his old home nestled in the Blue Ridge. On weekends he would stomp up the slopes of rocky overlooks along the Appalachian Trail. Once there he could see the countryside with its patchwork quilt of farms for 20 miles or more, but here in southern Georgia all he could see were treetops. And because of the hot weather and humidity he wore his boots with the laces untied at the top to allow a cushion of air to cool his feet. He replied, "They suit me well enough."

"You go sinking in the mud," said the elderly man, "and we might have to send an undertaker after you."

The good ole boys chuckled harder than ever.

Mike wondered whether their taunting would turn into something more dangerous if he had been born above the Mason-Dixon Line.

"Do you want to reconsider?" asked Sheriff Barnes.

Mike didn't trust them. And he could barely make out what they were saying because of their deep southern drawl. "I'm ready to go."

As they boarded the fan boat, the man with big arms said, "Shucks, boy, we were just funning you."

The next day Mike and his sister, Claire, launched their canoe. He sat in the stern and paddled. He was shorter than his brother, but had strong arms from lifting weights with him. Claire sat in the bow and scoured the swamp for any plants they could sell to local businesses for cash. Her brunette hair was shoulder length, curled from the humidity as though she had applied a styling gel. She snapped, "There's some ginseng," spotting a cluster of red berries. Mike paddled over and let the canoe float nearby. She plucked the whole plant with its roots, which she'd grind into medicine. Watercress grew wild. They picked some to sell to the organic restaurant. And they picked swamp candles, a plant with a spike-like cluster of yellow petals on its stem, to sell to the florist shop. They knew that some of the plants were protected by federal laws so they were secretive about where they traveled. Day after day they drifted farther from the canal into the canopy.

One day they drifted into a clearing of deep black water. They paddled toward a grove of cypresses on the far side of the swamp, hearing water lap against the canoe. A sneezy bark, *kee-yow...kee-yow*, came from nearby. Mike peered into the branches above with his binoculars and spotted a short-eared owl with luminous yellow eyes. The noise sounded like a warning, but they kept going. They saw a totem pole fastened to a tree. On the bottom was a carving of a python, then a black bear, a white-tailed deer, and on top an owl. He spotted what looked like a huge hammock suspended by ropes in-between two cypresses. "Stop," he screamed.

Claire grabbed a knobby knee sticking out of the water.

Mike saw a woman with long black hair and a boy with a tussle of hair hanging about his neck. Their bodies were sinewy and their skin shined reddish-brown.

The woman tied a rope ladder from the hammock to a knobby knee. She called out to them, "Eat with us." First the boy climbed the ladder, then the woman.

Mike tied the canoe to a cypress. They waded through knee deep water to the ladder. Claire climbed up. Mike followed.

Hanging up inside the makeshift home, made of intertwined vines and dried clay, were muskrat skins, deer hide, and a black bear pelt. The squaw brought out empty bowls. She placed a pot of steamy venison and squash on the floor and said, "Eat."

Mike and Claire dug into the meal, murmuring, "mmm." While they ate, they felt tension on the bottom of the canvass floor.

An Indian brave, who had black mud streaked down each cheek and looked as gruesome as a zombie raised during a voodoo ceremony, entered the room. He spoke, "I am Troy Black Snake. This is my wife, Ituha (sturdy oak), and son, Ahmik (beaver). We are Choctaw."

"Choctaw?" asked Claire. "I thought you lived on a reservation in Oklahoma?"

"Several of us skilled in the ancient arts of trapping and stalking game have fanned out over the south from the backwaters of the bayou to the swamps of the East Coast to ply our trade. That is how I provide for my family."

"Do you stay here all year long?" asked Claire.

"In the winter the hunting and weather is good. Not so in the summer. That is when we return to the reservation in Oklahoma."

Keith stared at him in disbelief. He shouted, "I know what you did!"

"I saved your brother's life," stated Troy Blake Snake.

"Saved his life?" gasped Keith. "You shot him with an arrow. He almost died on the way to the hospital."

"He was standing in knee-deep water next to a giant python."

"You could have shot the arrow into a tree," said Keith. "A warning shot!"

"I had to get him out of there as quick as possible."

"You are mad," blurted out Claire.

"Believe what you wish," said the brave. "You behave like newborn fawns. You see how beautiful the world is, but don't understand all its dangers."

Claire pushed her bowl aside and scoffed, "I'm not hungry anymore. Let's go."

They clambered down the ladder as fast they could. Mike untied the canoe and climbed in. They paddled away from the treehouse.

"I don't like the way he looked at us," said Claire.

"I didn't either," griped Mike.

They kept looking back to the treehouse to make sure Troy Black Snake wasn't shimmying down the ladder to follow them. When they got out of earshot, his sister said, "I've locked the GPS location into my cell phone. We'll report him to the police when we get back."

13

"I don't think Sheriff Barnes' fan boat can fit back here," said Mike.

"Not to that knucklehead," scoffed his sister. "To the state police."

They crossed a pond covered with green duckweed and zigzagged through a tangle of bushes, going a bit west of the treehouse. A thrush tweeted from a bush and a series of *hoo-hooaw's* sounded above. Mike peeked into the burlap bag and saw only $25 worth of trimmings. The moss surrounding a stunted oak shimmered lime-green and the bright spotlight of the sun cast golden tones upon the black water.

"Over there," snapped Claire, pointing to a small mound.

He had seen the splash of maroon color too. He steered them in that direction. They paddled forward with the water gurgling underneath the bow and slowed down within a foot of the mound. On the other side was deeper marsh with clumps of cord grass.

"Look!" gasped Claire. "We can get five dollars apiece for each one." She was pointing to a bunch of rare maroon orchids that had bloomed on the far side of the mound of twigs.

Mike stepped onto a patch of mud that was firm enough to support his weight and climbed onto the mound. He crawled over the twigs and reached down to pick an orchid. It smelled sweet and had a wonderful luster up close. He heard squeaking to his right and saw seven or eight gators no bigger than his hand on the other side of the mound. By then it was too late.

The patch of mud behind him moved and a monster gator rose up. Its shoulders were as broad as the biggest cypress and half its length was still hidden in the black water.

"Oh, God!" he screamed.

The gator opened its huge mouth and swallowed his right leg and arm. Its jagged teeth were about to clamp shut and rip him in half.

"No!" he yelled, thrusting his left boot in-between its lower jaw.

Its teeth got stuck on the leather boot, stopping its mouth from closing. The gator wiggled its body and clamped down again.

Mike pushed off with both hands to get his legs free. His left foot slipped out of the boot caught in the gator's teeth and his right foot sunk in the mud. "Help! Help!" he yodeled as panic shook his body.

Claire screeched and beat the gator's backside and tail with her paddle, but couldn't stop the monster from moving. She kept smacking the water after it had slithered farther toward him, splashing up waves.

The whole world seemed to be moving. The gator slithered toward him, his sister smacked the water, and even the trees and bushes appeared to be shifting.

Mike grabbed a branch floating on the surface and thrust it against the gator's snout. It crumbled apart, rotten to the core. He flopped backwards, trying to swim away.

The gator wagged its tail, propelling toward him.

Then he saw it. A canoe slicing through the black water, blending in with the scenery because it had been carved out of a sycamore, and the darkened face of Troy Black Snake. The brave catapulted himself into the water in-between him and the monster with only the long pole he used to power the canoe.

The gator lunged again, going vertical into the air. It slid up the pole, and its jagged teeth gleamed only inches away from the brave's face. The Indian flipped the gator back into the water. It rolled over and swam toward Mike again.

"Oh, no!" Mike tried to run away, sloshing through the water, but his boot sunk into the mud. He dove headfirst into the black swamp. He felt the creature slithering on top of him. He swirled around beneath the surface, blinded by debris rising up from the bottom. This was how he was going to die: by sucking water into his lungs or having the gator crunch his bones in its mouth. A series of events from his childhood to yesterday flashed in his mind like a movie reel. He felt its teeth ripping away his shirt and sinking into his flesh. He popped up to the surface and beat his arms against its snout. Pain pulsed in his ribs and a swirl of blood reddened the water like a psychedelic painting. The gator clambered over him, the weight of its body pushing him back underneath.

He saw the gator spinning in the swamp again and the pole pushing it away. Then the burly legs of Troy Black Snake stepped over his submerged body. The brave once again waded toward the creature.

Tilting his neck up, he broke the surface. Mike gasped for breath, spitting out water and muck. He held onto a cypress root to keep from being sucked back into the fray. He saw a brown cloud forming near the brave's legs and the ridges of the gator's back breaking the surface. While he trembled with fear, the brave rushed forward, prodding the gator with his pole. With each thrust the Indian's arms and back uncoiled with muscular power. Mike's shoulders bobbed up. He motioned toward the canoe and yelped, "Claire!...Claire!"

His sister's eyes were wide open and her mouth agape. Her frozen body did not move.

He cried out again, "Claire, get me out of here!"

His sister paddled toward him while from behind he could hear Troy Black Snake grunting and water splashing. Ripples spread out in a circle.

Claire came upon him and pulled him into the canoe.

Mike fell in the bottom exhausted and heaved several breaths.

She ripped a towel apart and wrapped the shreds around his waist. She declared, "You're all right."

Still drops of blood soaked through the bandage and his stomach throbbed.

Out in the swamp the gator swam back to its nest and crawled atop the mound. When the creature turned around, it dwarfed the Indian with its size. Troy Black Snake thrust the pole, keeping the gator away as its hisses filled the air and its gaping mouth showed rows of sharp teeth.

"You saved my life," shrieked Mike, who was in a state of shock.

"Get your stuff," snarled the brave, "and go."

They paddled over. Mike was covered with mud and dripping water. His sister grabbed the burlap bag.

"Don't you hear them?" asked Troy Black Snake.

There was a cacophony of chirps, croaks, and clicks coming from all around. Water drops plopped from a lily frond. *Hoohoo* came from above.

"Hear what?" asked Mike.

"They eat small game like mice, squirrels, and those baby alligators. When they perch in the canopy, predators such as pythons and alligators lurk below."

A subtropical bird cried from somewhere, *caw-ki-ki-ki*, and an insect rubbed its shell nearby, *rikki-rika-rika*. Bubbles percolated up from the bottom. *Hoohoo-hooaw*, sounded above.

"You mean..."

"Beware of the omen of the owl."

Don't Tread On Me

TIM TOM WONDERED HOW long were they going to keep singing. For the last ten miles, since they saw the mist hanging over the Blue Ridge, they had been screeching *We're here because we're here…* He wanted to say something, but only peeked in the rearview mirror. Iggy jangled a tambourine in the back seat and Blossom grinned from ear to ear as those words escaped her mouth. Ryan was the only serious one, hunkered down behind them checking the climbing gear. Tim Tom's wife, Mary, leaned closer and whispered, "We got to pick up dog food." He saw a sign that read *Green Spring Mills* as they rumbled over a set of railroad tracks into the town. Green Spring Mills had always been a crossroads between the coastal plain of Virginia and the Shenandoah Valley, between suburban gentry whose fingers tapped PC keyboards in high-rise office buildings in Richmond and plain country folk whose soiled-stained hands toiled in farm fields, a place rich in history because the mill made gunpowder for the confederates during the Civil War and Stonewall Jackson often bivouacked his troops there, a place where Independents outnumbered both Republicans and Democrats, where the local Baptist church held socials every month during winter and barbeques during summer, where bluegrass musicians gathered to pick banjos and pluck steel guitars, and where American flags flew from every other house though some hung upside down as a sign of protest.

"I'm itching to get into those hills," babbled Iggy, "and go spelunking."

"I ain't crawling into no holes," griped Tim Tom. "I've seen enough of them in Iraq looking for that bastard, Saddam Hussein."

"We had to do what we had to do," said Ryan, who looked thin enough to fit into a hole of any size.

17

"Come on, Tim Tom," chided Mary, "it will be fun."

"I'll spot you," he replied. "That's all I'll do. Someone's got to keep an eye on these dogs."

His Austrian shepherd, Oscar, was sprawled in the rear of the SUV over a tent bag, Ryan's white lab, Scout, peered out of a side window with a smile spread across his face, Iggy's dog, Max, half Rottweiler and half Ridgeback, was draped over his wife's lap, and Blossom's little bull terrier, Samantha, was wrestling with a coil of rope. Tim Tom spotted *Miller's*, a countrified version of 7-Eleven, on the right and turned into its gravel parking lot.

Everyone got out. Tim Tom leaned against the hood of the SUV and did a dozen pushups to keep in shape, not worrying about messing up his crewcut or clothes, while Mary brushed her curly brown hair in the window's reflection, Iggy slurped on an orange, and Ryan tethered the dogs to leashes. Blossom trotted them around the parking lot, being a perfect earth mother with a blouse of blooming flowers and her auburn hair braided into pigtails. The rest of them moseyed toward the front door.

A yellow flag, with part of a snake visible, drooped from a staff pegged in the wall. Ryan stopped and said, "I don't like the look of this. In Ben Franklin's day it made sense, but now?"

Tim Tom surveyed the street in both directions. "Where else are we going to go?"

"There's got to be a supermarket somewhere," said Mary.

"Not in a town this small," replied Tim Tom. "Let's go in and get what we need. We don't have to come back here."

When they rambled inside, a bald man with a set of keys clanking on his belt was fixing a pot of coffee and a kid in an apron stood behind the counter. The bald man twisted around and gave them a strange look. Was it their clothes? Tim Tom was wearing camouflage trousers and a tan T-shirt, Ryan a camo jacket and hat, and Iggy weaved in and out of the aisles wearing bell-bottom jeans and a Nehru jacket that combined with his long hair made him the spitting image of a new age guru. Tim Tom didn't know if the man would ask them why they were going deer hunting a week before the season opened or say something crazy like, *What's that jerk doing with you GIs?* They got powdered milk and flour for pancakes, canned tuna and a loaf of wheat bread, a packet of lean-cut meat, and Purina dog chow.

The teenage boy, who had zits on his face, rung up the items and placed them in a paper bag. "That will be $23.52."

Tim Tom handed him his credit card.

"This says your name is Timothy Thomas," chuckled the boy. "You have two first names. Didn't your mama know who the father was? Ggghhh!"

Tim Tom lifted him up by his shirt collar which tightened around his neck. "Apologize about my mother."

The boy's face turned pale and his feet kicked air.

"Put him down, Tim Tom, please," pleaded Mary. "You're hurting him."

Tim Tom set the punk down, whose face flushed beet-red.

"Jeffrey, I'll take care of this." The older fellow shooed him away.

The boy hunched over and gagged as he stumbled into a storage room.

"You must excuse him. He's wet behind the ears. So where are you folks heading?"

"Up to the Highlands."

"You here to join the militia?"

"No," said Tim Tom, "We don't need to join a militia. We served six years in the Marine Corps with two tours in the Gulf, including that guy." He pointed to Iggy.

The man looked back and forth between him and Iggy as though he didn't understand their connection.

Tim Tom remembered the day clearly. They hustled into an alley behind a market square in Fallujah to escape sniper fire. Two members of his squad were hit and howled in pain. A rat-a-tat-tat-tat pinned them down behind a wall as a row of insurgents opened up on their position. They couldn't move. A mechanical creaking came from the street. Then an armored personnel carrier squeezed into the alley. The Hodgies fired RPGs, rocket-propelled grenades, at the carrier, but it kept on coming. Someone inside countered-fired with a heavy machine gun, causing the Hodgies to change position. His squad hustled into the carrier, squatting while carrying their wounded comrades. Iggy sat behind the steering wheel with earphones blaring out Metallica. The other grunt shut the hatch. They began backtracking to safety with RPGs bouncing off its iron shell, the blasts blending in with the drumbeats and crashing cymbals of the music. Tim Tom said, "He helped us out of a jam."

The old man cringed as though he thought the jam might have something to do with a drunken binge somewhere.

Tim Tom sighed.

The grocer handed him a receipt. "You guys know trouble is brewing in the nation's capital. We'll need our militia to fix it." He still had that look on his face. It was the way a character would look in a Clint Eastwood spaghetti western with squinted eyes and scrunched up face, but there was no whistling in the background. Tim Tom knew he had seen that look before in real life, but couldn't place it.

"We're going spelunking," jabbered Mary, hoping to relieve the tension.

"Spelunking?"

"Yeah, spelunking," said Iggy. "It'll be awesome. They probably got caves up there bigger than the Luray Caverns."

"I don't know about caves." cautioned the man, "but if you go poking around in the Highlands, you better be ready to deal with our militia. They protect a treasure that belongs in a bank vault."

When they left the store, Mary was jittery. "Maybe we shouldn't do this. I didn't like the look on that man's face."

"Screw him," said Tim Tom. "I'm not scared by any look. We're here to go camping and we're going to enjoy it."

They chugged down Main Street where elderly porch sitters and tiny tots gawked at their load of dogs and the strange man in the Nehru jacket, rolled along an asphalt highway past pastures with herds of cows or horses hemmed in by barbed wire fences, and about four miles out of town turned off on a country road that wound through the foothills. The SUV's transmission strained going up the mountainside and its wheels spit gravel. The solid lines on the map gave way to dotted lines and they found themselves on a fire road that went past natural stone cairns on either side. They came to a trail across the mountain with pink squares marking the trees, causing Blossom to gush, "Those pink blazes are as lovely as flowers."

"Those blazes aren't pink," scoffed Tim Tom. "They're as red as a stop sign, but thunderstorms have worn off their color."

And everybody agreed that the Long Lost Trail had once been blazed bright red, perhaps as a warning to day hikers who didn't understand the demands of hiking along rocky footpaths on such steep slopes.

They parked the SUV and unloaded their backpacks. They hiked along the fire road, which became narrower and rockier. They heard automatic rifle fire in the distance…ping… ping…ping…and the sound of a machine gun…ch-ch-ch-ch-ch-pow! Tim Tom stopped and said, "The militia is up ahead."

"Look at these trees," gasped Mary, whose hand trembled.

A few oaks along the fire road had their bark shredded with bullets, with the fragments lodged deep inside the grain, like so many woodpecker holes.

"We better keep our distance," warned Tim Tom. "Let's try the Long Lost Trail."

They backtracked and begun again. They hiked along the Long Lost Trail through forests of striped maple and yellow pine, meadows blooming with alpine wildflowers, and rocky gorges known as the Devil's Run. They came upon cliffs studded with caves and explored each one. Mary was afraid they would wake up hibernating bears, but Tim Tom told her that the carnivores like tree cavities and caves in the Lowlands. The dogs guided them to each opening the way hounds led hunting parties to fox holes, and sometimes bats fluttered out in waves. Iggy hummed or sang as he lowered himself into each cavern. Most were small crawl spaces only five or six feet deep, but one cavern opened up to reveal a room with 20-foot high ceilings and lavish trimmings that appeared to be carved by running water. Another had a stately entrance supported by massive pillars reminiscent of a southern mansion. When they stood on its stone porch, they could see other mountains, in the distance, overlapping each other with a bluish tint.

Late that afternoon they hiked up the mountain until they reached its crest and pitched camp in a barren landscape with several stunted pine trees. Wind whipped off patches of snow while down below, in the valley, they could see a multi-colored forest, bejeweled with lakes that shone as brightly as sapphires. The contrast was grave, but it stirred excitement within Iggy who kept chattering about the joys of spelunking.

The women set up tents by a ledge that sheltered them from the wind while the men built a fire further out in the open. Tim Tom gathered branches broken off from trees and pressed them against his knee to break off huge pieces. He used a pair of metal tongs that Ryan had brought with him to put the logs in the pit. As the fire grew stronger and stronger, he added larger and larger pieces of firewood. He was carrying over a log when there was a loud bong…and the tongs snapped apart and it fell with a thud.

"What did you do?" gasped Ryan.

"I'm sorry about that," said Tim Tom. "Sometimes stuff like that happens."

"If you pick up logs weighing 60 pounds!" whined Ryan.

"How can you even lift that?" asked Mary.

"When you have 220 pounds of muscle and no fat, you can lift anything." Tim Tom hunched over into the classic crab or most-muscular-man pose, tightening his six-pack abs and making his biceps bulge.

"My fireplace tongs are ruined," lamented Ryan.

"Don't worry. I'll replace them," said Tim Tom, "…someday."

Mary laid out strips of steak on a tiny grill. Soon the juices splashed in the coals and a hearty aroma wafted into the air.

Iggy and Blossom trotted off by themselves and huddled underneath the stone ledge. Iggy rolled a joint as fat as a cigar, smoked it down half way and flipped it around.

"Shotgun that thing," yelped Blossom.

He placed the burning end in his mouth and blew out a stream of smoke from the other end.

Blossom inhaled and held her breath as long as she could, slapping the rocks with her hands. Then snot flew out of her nose, and she hacked and coughed. The exhaled smoke formed a plume that looked like a balloon. Afterwards, a big smile filled her face.

"You guys don't know what you're missing," called out Iggy.

"We don't want to know," said Ryan.

"That junk makes you weak," advised Tim Tom, "and gets you in trouble."

The couple kept on smoking until the joint burnt their fingertips and they were floating with the clouds. In the distance they saw a snow-capped peak, a crimson setting sun, and blue mist. Iggy pointed and said, "Look...same colors as in our flag."

"And not that silly yellow one outside the store," said Blossom.

They all ate the flank steak sizzled on the grill and potatoes that had been wrapped in tin foil and baked in the red-hot coals. Iggy boogied on a sheet of snow which crackled underneath his boots and banged on his tambourine, *I knew a man Bojangles and he'd dance for you in worn out shoes....*

Ryan and the women joined in, *with silver hair, a ragged shirt, and baggy pants...The old soft shoe. He jumped so high, jumped so high then he lightly touched down.*

Iggy sang about how the fellow ended up in jail in New Orleans and said his name was Bojangles and how the other inmates would call out...

And everyone shouted, including Tim Tom, *Mr. Bojangles, dance....Mr. Bojangles dance....*

For a few hours they sang songs on the mountaintop feeling the companionship that comes from camping together and being as close as any friends could be. When the fire died down to only embers and owls hooted...hoohoo...hoohooaw... from the valley below, they slipped into their sleeping bags and fell asleep.

A bit after sunrise they packed up their gear and hiked along the crest of the mountain, which was pockmarked worse than the Badlands out west. They came to an opening that looked promising enough to lead to an underground cavern. Water was dripping inside, possibly from snowmelt, which could mean mineral deposits had been shaped into statues. They put on their helmets and gloves and tethered a rope to a nearby boulder.

"Not so fast," shouted Tim Tom. When he yanked it, the hitch knot came loose. He wrapped the rope around the boulder again and secured it with a double-overhand knot. "Okay. Be careful." He grabbed the dogs by their collars and made them lay on the ground.

Iggy was the first one to drop down into the hole and disappear in the darkness. Blossom, Mary, and Ryan followed. They stomped inside without saying a word, stepping on something that oozed underneath their feet.

"Must be a ton of mud down here," muttered Blossom.

"Or moss," said Mary.

"I can flip on my light," suggested Ryan.

"Not cool," chided Iggy. "Let's wait until we get to the center. Then we can turn on our headlamps and be blown away by the stalactites and stalagmites."

They walked a bit further and heard a rattling sound echo off the walls.

"Iggy," asked Ryan, "is that your tambourine?"

"Yeah, I suppose it is," he said. "I still got it with me."

They heard it echoing more and more the farther they went. Mary thought *Maybe we're stepping on bags of gold coins* and got lightheaded and giggled with the fantasy of discovering the militia's treasure.

"We must be in an echo chamber," jabbered Iggy. "Cool."

They stopped at a place that was pitch-black without so much as a hint of sunlight coming in from above. Blossom asked, "How about here?"

"Go ahead everybody," declared Iggy.

They flicked on their headlamps and the beams converged to become as bright as a bonfire illuminating the cavern. All around them rattlesnakes were slithering on the floor, curled around rocks, and intertwined in mating configurations that would make Adam and Eve blush. Some were coiled in the classic rattler style which announced, *I'm going to fling myself at you and bite.*

The women screamed and Iggy turned to Ryan and started to say, "What are…" but before he could get the words out…his friend was a blur…sprinting out of the cave.

Tim Tom knew something was terribly wrong when he could hear the women screaming and Iggy calling his name. Before he could mumble, "What the…" Ryan came roaring out of the hole faster than an Amtrak train on a slick track and twirled around and yelled, "Get them off me!"

"Get what off you," wondered Tim Tom.

"Snakes! Hundreds of them are down there."

Tim Tom slid down to the bottom of the pit with his headlamp turned on and secured one end of a safety rope with a fireplace tong. Snakes were coiled near his feet and hissed from everywhere. He saw the group huddled on a ledge above the reptiles, gripping each other in terror. He plodded toward them with no feeling of panic inside. The cuffs of his jeans were tucked into his boots, which the snakes bounced off of, scratching the leather with their fangs. If one came near his body, he batted it away with the other fireplace tong. He jumped onto the ledge where they had taken refuge and fastened the safety rope with the other fireplace tong. He pulled safety harnesses out of his backpack and fastened them to the rope. Iggy and Blossom plopped into the seats and pulled themselves across the cavern above the snakes slithering down below. When they got near the cave's entrance, the rope started to fray. Tim Tom held on with all his strength, but it shredded apart. He and Mary were now stranded themselves.

Snakes were coiled like the image on the yellow Revolutionary War flag that read *Don't Tread On Me* and hissed loudly. Mary huddled against the cave wall and shivered in terror. Tim Tom crouched down and looked into her eyes and said, "Don't be scared by those rattlers. We got to go through them to get to freedom."

Mary nodded.

"Help me push this boulder off the ledge." Tim Tom leaned forward and pushed with both hands.

Mary pushed a little and gave up. "There's no way we can do it."

Tim Tom turned around and squatted, putting his feet against the base of the wall. He pressed his back against the boulder, leveraged his position with his thighs, and pushed. Crack…the boulder shifted and tumbled down…rumble…crash, crushing rattlers caught underneath and clearing a path to the rope. He draped Mary over his shoulder and carried her to the hole. With her clinging to him, he tried to climb up but was drained. He had nothing left, and the snakes were beginning to coil again near his feet.

"Come on, you guys," he yelled, "pull us up."

The gang above ground gave a half-hearted attempt, not lifting them an inch.

"We can't do it," said Iggy. "They're too heavy."

But Samantha, the tiny bull terrier, grabbed the rope in her teeth and pulled it taut. The other dogs came over and Ryan hooked the rope to their collars like a team of sled dogs and yelled, "Mush…mush!" The rope began to move…up…up…up…

"Let's put some backbone in it," yelled Ryan.

Everyone grabbed the rope and tugged. It moved upward even though the pair seemed to weigh a ton. After what seemed like forever, the two popped out of the hole. Ryan and Iggy grabbed Mary and laid her on the ground. Tim Tom shimmied out using his powerful legs and dropped his backpack to the side. Everybody was panting hard.

"We're lucky you were around, Tim Tom," said Blossom. "I hate to think what could have happened."

They heard something rattle.

"Iggy," quipped Ryan, "you must be happy to be shaking that…"

Then they all saw it. A snake had slithered out of the open backpack and was now coiled, ready to strike Mary in the arm or leg. Tim Tom had only seen sinister eyes like that once before…and now the memory flashed in his mind….on the face of an al-Qaeda terrorist attacking a checkpoint in Sadr City. The snake's mouth popped open and its body sprung forward as Mary jerked back in horror and a piercing scream flowed from her lips.

Thud…Tim Tom's boot came down in one swift thrust and crushed the snake's head against a rock.

"Oh, my…." gasped Blossom.

Their ordeal was over, but Ryan, who'd been creased by a snake's fang, vomited on the ground.

"We got to get him to a hospital," said Tim Tom as he unfolded a map of the mountain. "We can connect with the fire road here. Then follow that to our SUV."

They hustled along the Long Lost Trail for a half mile to another trail marked with yellow blazes and trudged toward a rocky spire that towered a thousand feet above. The closer they got, the clearer they could hear the ping…ping…ping of automatic rifle fire. The path rose upward through a wood of hemlocks so tall you couldn't see their crowns. Trees that were seedlings during the American Revolution, hundreds of years ago, now formed a wedge of massive old growth in the forest. Tim Tom thought about how we are all a part of nature, not independent of it, and that nature, itself, is greater than any individual person or thing just like society is. But the roots must have been deep because the ground was hard except for green lichen growing around the base of each trunk. They climbed closer and closer to the massive mound. The rifle fire stopped.

Everybody slowed down and looked about.

Another trail was marked with blue blazes. Tim Tom shook his canteen upside down and a few drops fell out. "This leads to a spring," he said, taking off in that direction.

Everybody followed.

The foliage became thicker and the air smelled damp. After 50 yards, they heard the trickling of water. They pushed back bushes thick with leaves and stumbled into a clearing with a spring that bubbled up from a subterranean pool. The dogs started lapping up water and little Samantha, the bull terrier, splashed about until Blossom dragged her away.

"Not so fast," warned Ryan. "There might be bacteria in the water."

"What are we going to do?" said Mary, looking worried.

"It can't be that bad," said Tim Tom. "We're out in the middle of nowhere." He bent over, scooped up the water in his palm and drank..."mmm"...

Everybody stooped over and took turns filling up their canteens or drinking from the spring with cupped hands.

Samantha was patrolling along the edge of the forest.

Tim Tom spoke, "I hear them."

"Hear what?" asked Mary.

"You'll see."

The sound of twigs snapping, as though deer were wandering through the forest, grew louder. Then they heard the breathing of guys humping with heavy packs on their shoulders. And finally branches broke off bushes, boots pounded dirt, and a yellow flag came out of the trees along with a half dozen scruffy guys with five o'clock shadow, dressed in old sweat shirts and shabby winter coats. A heavyset man with a roll of stomach hanging over his belt buckle strode forward and announced, "This here spring is claimed by the Sovereign Citizens of Green Spring Mills."

"No, it's not," objected Ryan, who unfolded a map. "It's within the boundaries of the National Forest."

The man swung an AK-47 toward him.

He froze in mid-scoop.

All the men were armed and now raised their weapons.

Blossom hugged Samantha as though she was her child.

"You can put them down," said Tim Tom. "We're about to leave."

"We can't let them go," said another. "They know where we are."

"We might know where you are," said Tim Tom, "but we don't care."

"What do you mean *you don't care*?" asked the rotund ringleader.

"We just went spelunking," jabbered Iggy.

"Who's this jerk?"

"Don't be getting hot under the collar," said Tim Tom, trying to defuse the situation. "We're taking my friend, Ryan, to a hospital. He got bit by a rattler."

Ryan lifted his pants cuff to show the bandage on his calf, which had swollen to twice its normal size.

"We can't let you go until Jacob says we can."

"Where's he?"

"You'll have to go with us and talk to him."

Tim Tom sized up the sorry troop before him and sighed. "Let's go with them. It can't be that far."

They trekked through the woods, breaking off branches, crushing plants with their boots, and getting stuck by thorny bushes. They came to the cliff face and stepped out of the darkness into bright sunlight and hit a wall of granite a hundred feet high.

"This ain't the way," said the fat guy.

They traced their way along the rim of the rock wall, going around boulders, stepping on stone ledges, and traversing an uneven, untrodden path. Buzzards circled overhead and swooped closer every time some fool stumbled. They came to an opening in the rock face, climbed up a dry streambed that only flowed after spring thunderstorms, and marched into a camp shielded by canyon walls, which kept most of the sound from automatic weapon fire confined within. The posse's leader huffed with exhaustion although the hike was only about a quarter mile. A motley crew stood before them in baggy hunter garb or blue jeans and sweats. Half the guys were holding cans or bottles of beer.

The leader of the militia was a thin man with a hideous smirk. Not a smile of joy, but with lips pulled taut. Jacob sneered, "Look at those guys. They're wearing fed uniforms."

"We served our country," said Tim Tom, "and moved back into civilian life like you."

"Not like me," he snarled. "I am a freeman. Free from the federal government and its IRS agents. Free from the president and the stooges in congress. Free from the federal judges who subvert the common law of the Republic and this here County."

The guys around him guzzled beer and grinned. A squad of marines could cut down this crew of fools in five minutes, thought Tim Tom.

"Only three things protect you in this world," announced their leader, "God, gold, and guns. Our families say their prayers every day. Our weapons are loaded and cocked. And we got enough gold to last until Armageddon." He ended his lusty sermon by drooling from the mouth.

"We believe in God like everybody else," replied Tim Tom. "And we can handle guns, but we ain't no gold bugs. We don't want what you have."

"No?" he asked. "Then why did you come here?"

"To go spelunking," said Iggy.

The man shook his head in disbelief. "I know what you're looking for."

"We're not looking for anything," said Tim Tom.

Jacob curled his index finger, "Come this way," and moved farther into the canyon with his guests following him. He stopped at an open pit with a rope ladder and gestured toward the bottom. "There is our treasure."

Tim Tom saw several crates labeled with signs for firearms and a steel lockbox with an iron padlock in the bottom.

The lining and bags around Jacob's eyes were dark and sinister. "You say you can shoot. Let's see if you can hit our target over there."

A militiaman tossed Tim Tom a 9mm Beretta Storm carbine and a clip. He had never used this brand of firearm before, but snapped the 20-round magazine in place like he was a pro. He thought it was a bit odd though that a group of guys who said they believed in what this

29

country stood for would buy all their weapons from Russia and Italy. The M-16 was as good as you could get, but this crap? About 30 yards away a target popped up. Inside the round ring was a photo of a man wearing glasses. Tim Tom hesitated.

"That's James Bartholomew, a damn liberal with the *New York Times*," snarled Jacob. "He writes articles about socializing health care. He wants to bankrupt our country."

Tim Tom peered down the sight and squeezed off a dozen rounds with rapid-fire precision. He ejected the clip and handed the firearm back.

"You didn't hit him once," laughed their leader. "There ain't no bullet holes."

"I hit what I aimed for."

There was a loud creak and the target bent forward. A militiamen went over and said, "Damn you, boy. You ruined our target." With one tap, it fell off the stand whose base had been riddled with bullets.

"I don't like the way you play, mister."

"I don't follow no rules," barked Tim Tom. "We're going."

"Not so fast," snarled Jacob. "Let's see what you can do with a Glock." He handed Tim Tom a Glock, pulled out another, and held it underneath his chin.

Another militiaman pulled on Mary's arm, "This way, lady," and escorted her to the target area.

"We're going to see if you can shoot as well as William Tell," said Jacob. "Put a beer can on her head."

Everybody started laughing. A couple fellows rooted around in a cooler full of melting ice and beer.

"How about this can of Pabst Blue Ribbon?" Iggy reached in and held it up. "It's got a ribbon he can use as a bull's eye."

"Iggy," warned Tim Tom, "don't give in to them."

Iggy chugalugged the brew and staggered toward Mary as though he was in a drunken stupor, leaning over to the left, almost falling, then tottering to the right.

"He doesn't know what he's doing," said Ryan, who sat on the ground with his wounded leg stretched out.

All the militiamen were laughing harder, and their rifles were either pointing at each other or up into the air. If someone accidentally pulled a trigger, there would be carnage everywhere.

Iggy was getting closer and closer to Mary.

Tim Tom was trying to figure a way out. Maybe he could reason with this fellow. "You got to let us go. If one of us get killed, the FBI will be swarming all over these hills."

"They'll never find us," bragged Jacob.

Iggy leaned backwards as though he was doing the limbo and then leaned toward Mary with the empty can.

"You better hold you head still, darling," said a militiaman holding an AK-47 at her.

Iggy fell face forward, putting his hands on the ground, and whipped his feet to the right, knocking the militiaman off balance.

"Aughh!" The fellow cried as he fell toward the ground.

Iggy wrestled the AK-47 away and bounced up. He spun and lay down a thread of bullets at their feet. Pop, pop, pop, pop...

The militiamen scattered.

Ryan and Blossom let loose the frenzied dogs, who were baring their fangs and frothing at the mouths like a pack of wild wolves. The dogs chased the militiamen through rock crevices and around boulders, biting their arms or legs to pull them down. Their growls were mixed with cries of pain.

Tim Tom twisted the leader's wrist, making his gun fall with a thud. He lifted the man up over his head and plodded toward the pit.

"Get your hands off me," hollered Jacob. "I'm the sheriff of Green Spring Mills."

Tim Tom pushed the man backwards.

He landed in the bottom of the pit.

"Now you got all the guns and gold you want," said Tim Tom.

"Down you go," said Iggy who had rounded up the others.

They skedaddled into the pit, stepping on the lockbox whose contents rattled.

"Pull up the ladder," ordered Tim Tom.

Iggy pulled it up.

"You can't leave us here," cried their leader.

"The hell we can't," said Tim Tom. "You'll figure a way out…someday."

The militiamen tried to climb up the clay wall with their bare hands, but slid back to the bottom. They kept on coming and coming - slithering against the wall, writhing against each other, and hissing threats at Tim Tom and Iggy.

"We'll get you." "We'll kill both of you." "We'll break every bone in your bodies."

"Let's go," said Tim Tom.

The women and dogs hurried down the dry streambed. Iggy skipped behind them, shaking his tambourine. Tim Tom helped Ryan hike out of the canyon loaded down with the backpacks. They retraced their steps to the spring and to the fire road. They hustled down to the SUV and threw their stuff in the back. When they pulled out, the tires spit gravel.

In a few minutes they were speeding down the highway toward the hospital. Mary turned around in the front seat and asked, "Iggy, I've never seen you act like that before. What got into you?"

The tambourine stopped jingling and his grin faded. He replied, "I can sober up pretty quick when my friends or country is on the line."

The Storm

CONRAD WAS WOKEN BY the sound of wind whistling under the eaves of the house and waves rolling into the shore, making him wary of the upcoming weather. He flipped on the lamp and peeked at the clock.

3:46 A M

Even though he had another 15 minutes to snooze, he rocked himself into a sitting position on the bed. His wife was asleep under the blanket, already used to him getting up. He trudged to the dresser, put on his pants and shirt, and flicked off the lamp. He shuffled into the kitchen and stuffed a muffin in his mouth. Washing it down with a few swallows of orange juice, he nourished himself for what was to come. He pulled on his hip waders and stomped out the backdoor.

Stars smoldered in the black sky and waves lapped at the boats moored to the dock. Wind ruffled his blonde hair, which fell in his eyes.

He tread on the wood planks as a handful of watermen were getting their vessels ready to sail. Every muscle in his body ached from the day before, yet he ventured forth toward the Lady Rebecca. What choice did he have? A dozen creditors were circling over his uncle's business, which he'd been running and was now closed. He needed to put food on the table.

"Morning," grunted the skipper on board.

The Lady Rebecca slipped out of the inlet and past the shoals near Hooper Island as a luminous glow rose over the Earth's arc on the eastern horizon and blotted out the stars. Gliding past the mouth of the Nanticoke River and Deal Island, the sunrise cast its pink light across the water. Still the skipjack sliced toward the Chesapeake Bay. Conrad saw a flock of pelicans skirting an island full of marshes and more open water. He wondered why the skipper didn't prepare the nets for fishing or point to a line of crab cages that needed to be hauled up. The other mate sat on the cabin with his back toward him.

"Storm coming," said the skipper.

The seawater was turquoise and the sun shined off its surface, creating a field of sparkling diamonds. Conrad didn't see any storm clouds. Off on the starboard side he noticed a wisp of gray fog, but that was it.

The skipper spun the wheel, and the craft turned to the right. The Lady Rebecca bobbed on the growing swells. Then Conrad saw it - a front of purplish-black clouds with lightning bolts appearing like flashes of fireworks. The swifter the wind blew and the choppier the swells became, the more treacherous it was walking on deck. Whitecaps, like so many surfing waves, broke on the surface near the skipjack. He wondered how he had gotten into this situation since he could barely swim. Then the reason came to him in one name - Zoe.

Conrad met her while moonlighting as a waiter at Dino's Bistro. He was an assistant manager at a burger chain, but wanted extra money for a down payment on a Lexus. A girl walked in with skin the color of baked bread and eyes like a doe. He stopped by the nearest mirror to check his hair and straighten his jacket. Zoe for her part made sure to ask for help carrying extra trays to a table or for him to fill in for the wine steward, who always happened to be on a break. They served delicacies such as shish kebab on pilaf and roasted lamb wrapped in grape leaves. Even though he had a relationship with a stocky girl of German heritage named Odette, who was always thoughtful and logical, something was missing. So he asked Zoe out on dates. At first they watched movies, then went dancing, and finally he took her to a Yanni concert in Washington D.C. All night, he stole glances at her in-between concertos composed for strings such as violin and cellos, contemporary jazz-styled arrangements with a robust brass sound, and serene ballads that the musician played on the piano.

Yanni was a magician at the keyboards whether playing piano or synthesizer and a master of orchestration, often prancing across the stage and making gestures to encourage the musicians to perform their best. Yanni smiled as he played the keyboards and swiveled his head of disheveled black hair, absorbed by the passion of the music, bounced up and down to the rhythm of an up-tempo song, closed his eyes during serene passages, and conducted the orchestra while drifting from piano to synthesizer and back again.

At the end of the concert the orchestra performed *The Storm*. The song started simply with a long orchestra passage called a ritornello because it would be repeated throughout after solo passages. The ritornello consisted of string music from violins, cellos, and a harp which reflected the sweeping wind and rainfall of the storm. Then the drummer pounded the kettle drums with batons to sound like thunderclaps, causing fans in the audience to bounce up and down to the rhythm. Two musicians popped up and performed a passage of dueling violins with the intensity and high-pitched sounds showing the storm's energy and plucked the strings to sound like raindrops falling. Fans were giggling and wiggling with delight, including Zoe. The full orchestra came back in with the ritornello and the bongos pounded and the drums boomed. The audience stood up and weaved back and forth to the sweeping tunes. Finally, the dueling violins took front and center and a frenzy of fireworks blasted behind the orchestra.

Realizing the concert was over, Conrad hugged Zoe and declared, "I love you."

Yanni strutted forth, turned his back to the audience, and bowed to the orchestra. The orchestra, in turn, bowed to him and an audience wild with delight. It was a memorable moment whether the storm was real or not.

Soon after that, they started sleeping together. And only four months after they had met, they were married. They settled in a five-room bungalow in the foothills of the Catoctin Mountains. One day Conrad walked outside their little home and found all his old CDs crushed into pieces and clothes he had left at Odette's apartment, including a new suit, cut to shreds with a scissors. His ex-girlfriend had become unhinged and possessed by a multi-headed dragon called jealousy. It was a bit after this that Zoe received word that her Uncle Philipp had had a stroke. So they took turns driving the Lexus 200 miles to Maryland's Eastern Shore.

They drove across the four-mile span of the Bay Bridge and down Route 50, which cut through small towns and large farms. After driving through Cambridge, they took a right on Route 16 and headed east. They passed by more farms and swampy terrain packed with wild ducks and geese. They crossed a rickety wood bridge and drove onto

Hooper Island with the inlet on one side and the Chesapeake Bay on the other. They pulled into the gravel parking lot of her uncle's restaurant, the Nicodemus Café, and walked up to the front door. It was locked. The couple peered through the glass and saw a half dozen round tables with wood chairs set upside down on top. They went next door to her uncle's house. When they entered the bedroom, he saw Zoe's uncle lying in bed. His wife, Helene, who had bushy eyebrows and salt and pepper hair that hung to her waist, sat beside him. On a seat nearby was Cousin Argo, who had arrived from the seaport of Larisa, Greece. Cousin Argo had a wide face, walrus mustache, and short hair that hung like a black mop on his head.

"Uncle Philipp," said Zoe, "this is my husband, Conrad."

Her uncle mouthed some words, but Conrad couldn't hear him. Zoe said he was glad to meet him. They talked for a few minutes with Zoe interpreting what her uncle said. Then Zoe stood next to him and asked, "What do you think?"

"We can put him in a nursing home," replied Conrad.

Zoe grimaced and shook her head. She announced, "We'll move down here and take over his business."

That was it. Zoe was a chameleon of moods, conveying them through a posture, pose, or pout. Conrad knew he could either obey her or lose her. "Sure," he agreed, "We'll take over his business."

Cousin Argo stood up, pulled out his wallet, and pinched a wad of cash in-between his fingers. "Let me give you money to take care of moving expenses. I will send more when I go home."

"Keep it," replied Conrad. "You are a guest in this country. Enjoy yourself. And keep your money when you go back home. We'll make do."

"You are a true man," said Argo, slapping his back. "This calls for drinking and dancing."

Aunt Helene went into the kitchen and returned with a dark green bottle. She squirted grappa into three shot glasses. The three men lifted their glasses and swallowed.

The grappa had the perfume of grapes, but a sharp alcohol bite that burned Conrad's throat. Still gasping for breath, he and Argo helped the old man up on his feet.

"Dance! Dance!" yodeled Aunt Helene.

Conrad and Argo held Zoe's uncle up and kicked out each leg in turn while her uncle kicked out his good leg. After a few minutes, sweat poured off Conrad's brow and he became weary. Aunt Helene played an old record on the stereo, and the men drank more shots and danced. Conrad couldn't remember anything after the third glass of grappa. He woke up by Zoe the next morning, unsure of how he had gotten to bed. They returned home with a plan in place.

Back in western Maryland they received threatening phone calls at night from an anonymous caller and were victims of small acts of vandalism that Conrad believed were carried out by Odette. They called 911, but the police said no action could be taken without proof. One morning he went outside and saw graffiti spray-painted on the side of the house questioning his wife's integrity by calling her a "bitch" and "whore". It took him an entire Saturday to scrub the siding clean. He wondered how many more heads of the green-eyed monster would rise from the depths of a scorned woman. Worried about Zoe's safety; he quit his job, helped Zoe to pack, and gassed up the Lexus. He drove the entire distance to the Eastern Shore while Zoe hummed along to tunes they heard on the radio.

They settled in a back room of Uncle Philipp's house. When Conrad looked out the window, he could see waves rolling into shore and seagulls scattering everywhere. It looked pleasant enough, but now the sea roiled its contempt and the sky spit in his face.

Usually the swells would be two to three feet in an unsettled sea, but Conrad saw breakers rolling toward the skipjack that were six to eight feet tall.

"Baton down the sails, lads," screeched the skipper.

Conrad and Ward dropped the mainsail and tied it to the boom. They skedaddled into the bow and dropped the jib. The rollers were now four to five feet high and the sky crackled with lightning above. Ward looped a rope around Conrad and tied a sailor's knot.

"What's this for?" he asked.

"Hold tight, landlubber."

A swell broke across the bow like a wave over a surfboard, showering seawater on everything in the boat.

Conrad slipped on the slick deck as the seawater drained out. He caught the rail and pulled himself upright, gasping for breath.

The skipper muttered, "Come on, lady."

"Come on, lady," called out Ward in a clearer voice.

Conrad huffed in utter panic, "Come on, lady…Come on, lady…"

Another wave broke over the bow, washing his feet from under him. In that moment, Conrad saw the mainsail go by and felt the boat moving ahead without him. He swam in the water as hard as he could, trying to keep from being washed overboard. The tether tugged on his stomach, pinching his body until it throbbed in pain. As the seawater drained out, he found himself sprawled in the stern, spitting salty foam from his mouth. It felt as though his waist had been stabbed by a hundred daggers. He couldn't regain his footing.

Ward clambered into the stern and lifted him up by the shoulders in the same way he emptied a crab cage. The mate thrust him against the railing and screamed, "Hold on!"

Another wave broke across the port side. This time the seawater drenched him, but flowed by without sweeping him off his feet. Both Ward and the skipper held fast without slipping away.

The Lady Rebecca sliced through the swells and stayed on course even though the storm swirled around her. Waves broke across her bow and rain lashed her battened down sails, causing the vessel to bob like a cork on top of the watery depths that could become their graves.

"Damn that Zoe," seethed Conrad. Then he recalled the series of events that unraveled his life on the Eastern Shore.

After Cousin Argo returned to Greece and Uncle Philipp began sitting up in a wheelchair and taking care of himself, it was like a second honeymoon for them. Conrad and Zoe opened up the Nicodemus Café during the week, and a few locals would stop in for breakfast and lunch, spending up to an hour or more eating and chatting. Then they opened the restaurant on a Saturday evening. Tourists visited the island and filled up several tables. In-between services and late at night Conrad and Zoe took romantic walks along the shore. They would hold hands, and he would gaze into the depths of her big doe eyes and profess his love for her. Hand holding led to hugging and attempts at baby making. One week the walk-in refrigerator went on the fritz. Conrad called a repairman who wanted $1,000 to get it running, but gave no guarantee his patch job would last more than a month. Conrad and Zoe looked at the old stoves and ovens used to cook dishes and knew the place had to be refurbished. So they decided to take their cooking on the road and introduce a new generation to Greek cuisine.

They traveled to folk art festivals in Easton and Salisbury, a beach festival in Ocean City, carnivals and fairs held in rural towns with only one or two stop lights along Main Street. They set up a stand along the side of Route 50 near Cambridge with pit beef and mutton roasting on spits. They sold gyros seasoned with tzatziki sauce made from yogurt, fresh cucumbers, and wine vinegar and wrapped in pita bread. They toiled for seven days a week for two months. One day Conrad pulled out two large stacks of money from the safe that were too big to wrap his hands around. He took the cash to the local bank on a Friday afternoon and deposited over $34,000. When they got home, he broke out a bottle of vintage chianti and Zoe jitterbugged to a Yanni CD. Soon they were drinking and dancing with Uncle Philipp and Aunt Helene sipping wine and clapping the beat. Several neighbors stopped by to see what was going on and joined in the celebration.

The following Wednesday Conrad went to the bank to withdraw cash to pay off the farmers who had been providing produce. The bank teller said, "I'm sorry, Mr. Wagner. Your account is frozen."

"What do you mean frozen?" asked Conrad. "I deposited over $34,000 last Friday. I want to see the manager."

The teller called over the manager, who strolled behind the counter and peered at the computer screen. He said, "Mr. Wagner, the IRS has put a hold on your account."

"I paid my taxes!" screeched Conrad.

"There's nothing I can do," stated the manager. "You have to take it up with them."

A week later Conrad had hired a lawyer, and they met with Judge Thornton in the circuit court of Dorchester County. Conrad took the stand and pledged to tell the truth. He explained to the judge how they had been visiting every venue they could to earn money and were working seven days a week. He said they were too busy to make periodic deposits.

A Department of Justice lawyer cross-examined him. He asked, "Mr. Wagner, do you know Argo Nicodemus?"

"Yes," answered Conrad, smiling at his wife. "He's our cousin."

The DOJ lawyer handed him a mug shot of cousin Argo, whose eyebrows drooped with his mouth and mustache. He said, "The Greek government has charged Argo Nicodemus with smuggling." He explained how the smuggling ring had been putting Syrian refugees on rafts and helping them to cross the Aegean Sea from Turkey to Greece. He then accused Conrad of laundering money from the smuggling operation through the local bank.

Judge Thornton banged the gavel and declared, "The defendant's bank account will be frozen until the DOJ and IRS complete their investigation. Counselor, how long will that take?"

"Three to six months," stated the DOJ lawyer.

As the government's lawyers swaggered out of the courtroom, Conrad said to his lawyer, "I didn't do nothing. I'm not a smuggler."

"They are not confiscating your money based on guilt," replied his lawyer, "but on *suspicion* of committing a crime. You are a victim of government overreach."

That weekend they sat in the house without talking. Zoe found a job at a local gift shop sewing bibs and aprons featuring an image of a crab. Conrad plodded down to the dock and joined the crew on the Lady Rebecca. His first day out the skipjack sailed south. They hauled up crab cages from Pocomoke Sound, dumping the cargo in the hull. The next day the skipjack crossed the bay to the mouth of the Rappahannock River. They cast the net, pulling up a dozen black drums with each sweep of the vessel. At the end of the day they had filled most of the hull with the huge zebra-striped fish. The work was hard, and he trudged home after each voyage with weary feet. The only spray that came on board the Lady Rebecca was from the swells it cut through. But now the sky was pitch-black and the whole vessel cracked as though the boards in the hull were about to break apart.

The skipjack seesawed from side to side, being pitched by the swells. Everything was enveloped in darkness as though a cloud had dropped on them. Conrad couldn't see his hands in front of him much less than the other crew members. Lightning rattled overhead as each board in the hull creaked in pain.

"Lord, have mercy on us," he pleaded.

The swells rolled forward and the wind swooshed as though the entire Earth was breathing. He expected the skipjack to be swallowed at any moment.

The seawater slithered around the vessel like a serpent and the rain fell down on them in huge drops, drenching everything on the deck. The Lady Rebecca sunk lower. They were in the belly of an ancient beast called death. All the timbers shook underneath his feet. Conrad's life flashed by as though on a film and he glimpsed Zoe for the last time. He waited for the final reckoning.

Then he saw that more spray was coming up over the bow from the Lady Rebecca slicing through the swells than rain falling from the clouds above. A yellow orb glowed up ahead and the skipper yelled, "Easy now, lady."

The creaking of her mast lessened and the cracking of her hull stopped. She would not break apart today. The swells decreased in size from four to three to two feet. Before long they were skipping through calm water with the sun shining overhead.

"Raise the sails, lads," ordered the skipper.

Conrad and Ward unfurled the mainsail and hoisted it aloft, straining when pulling on the wet ropes. They unfurled the jib.

Soon the Lady Rebecca picked up speed, running at close to 12 knots. Dolphins appeared off the sides and glided along. Conrad could see them breaching the waterline and breathing through their blowholes.

"Skipper, I see a pod forming up ahead," said Ward.

"Aye," said the skipper, who steered the skipjack in a wide arc.

"What's going on?" asked Conrad.

"The dolphins are swimming in a circle and rounding up a school of fish," observed Ward. "We are staying back until the right time."

Conrad could see bubbles coming up to the water's surface as the dolphins drew a circle tighter and tighter until it was no more than 50 feet in diameter.

"Get ready, lads," barked the skipper.

Conrad and Ward untangled the net on the port side and draped it along the rail. The Lady Rebecca veered to the left and cut across the circle. They dropped the net. After the vessel passed through, they tugged on the lines. The net was so heavy with fish it took all of their might to bring the load on board. Hundreds of mackerel swarmed inside, forming a silvery-blue ball. They loaded the catch into the hull.

The Lady Rebecca made three more runs across the tightening circle. Once they had to free a dolphin caught up in their net. The catch filled the hull. In a half hour they had caught the amount of fish they usually did in an entire day.

The skipjack turned and headed back to Hooper Island though how the skipper could tell which direction to go Conrad didn't understand. The water was smooth and the sailing was easy. Conrad saw an osprey diving into the bay and coming up with a fish caught in its beak, causing him to lean over the rail and leer because he knew they were getting closer to land. A swarm of seagulls wheeled in the sky and a pearly mist lingered on the horizon. He saw the lime-green of a field and a tan hill covered with wild grass. Tears welled up in his eyes and fell on his cheeks.

They dropped the sails as the Lady Rebecca glided into the inlet. Ward hopped onto the dock and tied her to the moorings. All three of them unloaded the catch and placed the mackerel in tubs that were hauled to the seafood packing company. When Conrad walked down the dock and placed his feet on solid ground, he sighed with relief. It felt good having firm footing underneath his shoes.

The Lady Rebecca went out two more days that week and passed through more storms, but Conrad learned how to keep hold of the rail to avoid slipping on deck and the other crew members seemed calm. Conrad didn't know if he had gotten used to bad weather or whether these storms were less severe.

On Sunday morning Conrad and Zoe entered a little white church that had a small steeple, gold-painted cross, and room for 150 people though only half that number showed for the service. They congregated with the other crew members, who sat silently with their wives. There was a gentle rustling as parishioners gathered in the pews and took out bibles. Conrad knew that a lot of people believed that this is where someone could find God. They were content to sit there and wait for the preacher's words to fill the church. But he now believed that God was found outside this place on the open water of the Chesapeake Bay. When he saw the splendor of the sunrise casting rays on the water's surface or dropped a net and pulled up a catch of teeming fish or cut through a squall on the Lady Rebecca, he realized that something greater than a mere man had created this world. He found God where he heard the wind blowing and felt the swells of the water…out where the Earth breathes.

Kerry and the Keys

UNCLE JACK KNEW HE could hold onto his dream of wealth for up to an hour or until the aftertaste was gone. It only took four belts of the hard stuff. The big score was still eluding him. For 30 years he had dived into every type of gambling: the roulette wheel, dice, card sharking, betting on horses, and now the managing of a Goth band. He formed the group for his niece, Kerry. With their first gig falling on Halloween, Kerry dyed her hair, painted her fingernails, and smeared her lips jet-black to appear as ghastly as a ghoul. She could sing the heck out of anything and a popular keyboardist named Sebastian had just left rehab. Sebastian sported a black van dyke beard and donned a dark habit to resemble a priest during the Spanish Inquisition. He was twice as old as his niece and had seen his share of painful death. When his hands crawled across the keys of a Moog Synthesizer, it seemed as though the theme from a Dracula or Frankenstein movie played. He performed the pieces in the key of C minor and included an odd assortment of sounds such as tubular bells, screechy violins, gong banging, hammer blows, and a shrieking cat. If he played a song in a higher key, it sounded as though someone was ascending the steps toward an attic where a mad woman gripping an axe waited. Which made their band, *Kerry and the Keys*, a smash with the kids. However, after two months of gigs their playing became sluggish and Uncle Jack's dream of making money from them was evaporating.

On this night the band rolled through their songs out of sync. Bruce, with his bulging biceps, beat the drums with so much force it sounded louder than the rumbling of an earthquake and the clashing of a thunderstorm, causing the whole stage to tremble. Lola, in her little black dress, flirted with the guys in the front row and squeezed the neck of the lead guitar so tight it screeched out notes. And Sebastian banged on the keys with his palms in a fit of anger. Consequently, the noise was worse than that coming from a construction site and drowned out his niece's singing. Uncle Jack stepped outside the stuffy bar to relieve his numb ears and smoke a cigar. A line of girls clad in miniskirts and designer jackets puffed on cigarettes with their backs toward him. They reminisced about the band as though it was a relic from the past:

"The band's not what it used to be," said one.

"I remember when they were hot," said another.

"She used to be the opening act for *The Lost Incas* and *Sunrise Beat*, but now..."

"...she can't even open a can of peas," interrupted Uncle Jack in anguish.

"Yeah," chimed the girl. "They can't even open a can of peas."

Uncle Jack twisted the stub of his cigar into the ground. He was a man in his 50s with a large pouch for a belly, round face, drooping chin, lackluster brown eyes, and slicked-back white hair. He shuffled backstage and critiqued the band's set, "To get a music contract we need to develop a unique sound or gimmick to draw in more fans. Then the music companies will be beating at our door."

"Wasn't that what you wanted?" asked Kerry.

"This band has to evolve," he said.

"How?"

"Turn down the volume."

A few days later the band held a practice session in an abandoned warehouse on the poor side of town. Uncle Jack hooked up an electric cord to a light pole so they could power their amplifiers and mic. In between songs, Kerry's younger sister Erin scared the heck out of the friends and groupies who milled about. Erin had a button nose and auburn hair that fell in swirls about her shoulders. She fancied herself to be a Celtic goddess born in a grove of oaks so she braided a lock on one side to resemble a vine. Since her spirit was as bold as Brigid, the goddess who collected the lightning to create fire, she snuck up on people and stomped her boots behind them to create the staccato sound of thunder. One man jumped in fright and fell into a bunch of boxes. Another shrunk to half his size in a protective crouch, afraid of being struck by a thunderbolt. While her sister sung the songs, Erin tramped about and mouthed the words.

Toward the end of the session Nathan Honeycomb, the guitarist for *Sunrise Beat*, barged into the band's practice. He looked like he was dressed for the beach with baggy white pants and an old suit splattered with multicolored patches, and his curly hair fell to his shoulders and his skin shined with a steadfast tan. He jabbered, "Like last week we were at the Galaxy Lounge doin' our gig and everyone was howlin' and I pulled out my Fender and…this seems crazy, man…laid on the floor and plucked sounds like whales floppin' in the shallows… and I rolled onto one shoulder and screamed, "Hey, Sebastian," and this guy, here, jumped onto the stage to jam with us…so here I am to show you how it's done."

He slung a guitar over his shoulder and plucked a pulsating rhythm which filled the hall. Sebastian played a funky arrangement with his fingers zigzagging across the keys. And Bruce pounded the drums and worked the cymbals. The music, which sounded similar to reggae with a touch of hard rock mixed in, caused people to squirm. Erin slipped off her jacket and swiveled her torso and high-stepped to the beat. Other people bumped butts and grinded on the cement floor. It seemed that the music would go on forever, but 10 minutes in…

Rumble. Rumble. Crash.

Grins turned into frowns. People asked them to lay down another tune, but Nathan was already packing up his guitar. Uncle Jack went over and asked, "Nathan, why don't you join our group? The sound is fresh."

"I've got a band, man."

"You can play for *Sunrise Beat* and *Kerry and the Keys*. We'll work out a schedule for you."

"Please, Nathan," begged Kerry. "We would love to have you play with us."

"Sorry, babe," he said, "I don' look good in black."

As he slinked out of the warehouse, Uncle Jack said to Kerry, "We'll have to find another way to make the band popular."

Kerry spent the rest of the week either pushing her band in relentless rehearsals or sprawled out on the sofa in her home reading music magazines. On Saturday morning a loud rapping rattled the door. When she opened it, Uncle Jack strutted in, lugging a steamer trunk.

"Are you going somewhere?"

"Not me."

"Me?"

"No," he laughed. "Maybe to Hollywood one day."

He dropped the dolly, and the steamer trunk landed with a thud. It was at least four feet long and had tiny holes drilled through the top. "I know how your mother feels about gambling, but I won something for you in a poker game. Do you like animals?"

She sprung into the air. "You got me a pet for my sixteenth birthday?"

"Yes, I did." He unlocked the box and flipped the lid.

A pair of paws gripped the edge and what appeared to be a large tabby cat poked its head over the side. The cat had a pink nose, translucent green eyes, which Kerry thought were more enchanting than emeralds, and solid black ears. The animal snarled and flashed its ivory fangs, which would make any ordinary person take a step back, but Kerry rushed toward the yawning animal with a delightful cry, "It's an ocelot." She pulled the cat out of the box. Three or four times bigger than an ordinary house cat, its white hide was covered with tan blotches enclosed by black rings. She hugged the critter so hard the hair on its neck fluffed up.

Uncle Jack beamed like a proud parent, "He can be the band's mascot. We'll call him *Montezuma*."

"I guess we can give him a home, but what happens if we can't afford to feed him? I'm not making any money with the band and mom hasn't got a pay raise in three years."

"If it doesn't work out, I'll cut off the cat's paws and sell them for 50 bucks each. A collector might buy its fur coat for another 500."

"How can you think of doing such a thing?"

"Of course, I'm kidding," laughed Uncle Jack. "He'll be a big draw at your shows."

Montezuma ruled his small domain until he was packed into the steamer trunk and dumped in the back of a rented truck along with the Moog Synthesizer, guitars, and drum set. They drove across town in stop-and-go traffic, jostling everything about, and parked at the warehouse while the band piled in amplifiers, speakers, and a bunch of unmarked boxes. Then they pulled in front of Sebastian's apartment building. They rambled down a stairway into the basement and knocked on a cold steel door. The latch creaked. Sebastian had dark eyes and spoke in a grim tone, "Do you have him?"

"He's right here," said Uncle Jack, pointing to the steamer trunk.

"Bring him in," ordered Sebastian.

They stepped inside the living room which was lit by a single candle. Sebastian shouted, "Bring him over here."

They lugged the steamer trunk over to a wood door. Sebastian opened the door to reveal a darkened room possessed by a huge dog whose growls were sinister and whose pointed white teeth gleamed about three feet above floor level. They unlatched the trunk and pushed the ocelot into the room. Sebastian shut the door. They heard barking and snarling and the animals being knocked against its walls. It went on for about 15 minutes when Sebastian said, "That should be enough time."

When the ocelot emerged from the room, it arched its back, with its fur sticking straight out, and hissed in menacing tones. They loaded the steamer trunk back onto the truck and drove to the nightclub with the band members being fully united.

At the nightclub Uncle Jack set up a folding table in the front lobby to sell the band's CDs and T-shirts. Each shirt featured Sebastian behind his keyboard and farther behind him stood Kerry singing into a mic. Both of them wore black from head to toe with Sebastian looking like a wizard and Kerry a witch.

Backstage, the band members lounged in chairs. Sebastian fished a discarded cigarette butt from an ashtray, relit it, and scratched his long hair which was tangled in knots. Although he always seemed as nervous as an electrician repairing a high-voltage wire, he stroked the keys with ultra-coolness. Already a legend, he joined his first band when he was a kid in grade school banging out renditions of Deep Purple's *Smoke on the Water*. He had learned all the tricks of the master keyboardists from Johann Bach to Rick Wakeman. When they stormed out of the dressing room and took over the stage, he strolled out to his Moog Synthesizer.

Bruce drilled the drums with rapid-fire precision while Lola whipped the lead guitar to provide a tight melody, but Sebastian played in a smooth predictable groove. The audience, made up of guys in dark leather jackets and ladies in sleek, but understated outfits, surged forward. Taunted by strange-looking freaks thrusting their hands toward him or spraying him with beer, Montezuma snarled and snapped his teeth.

Sebastian fingered the keys of the Moog Synthesizer in a slow movement in the key of A flat to make it sound as though birds were wheeling and squawking in the sky.

Montezuma reared up on his hind legs to claw the empty air. Fans pointed at the ocelot and jeered.

Then Sebastian's fingers moved quickly on the keys as more birds joined the covey with wrens, nightingales, owls, falcons, hawks, eagles, and even a condor joining the fray. He played their shrill cries in the key of F minor as the ball of birds circled in on each other in a frenzy - pecking, biting, clawing, and devouring their kind in wicked madness. The throng of spectators shifted to Sebastian's side of the stage.

The ocelot kept leaping into the air and clawing at the birds wherever they were. Then the cat crouched down in total confusion, swiveling his head every which way.

And Kerry did everything she could to scream out the lyrics above the carnage. Sebastian ended the song with the crunching of bones and the gurgling of blood.

The nightclub's owner told Uncle Jack, "Except for Sebastian, it's pretty lame. Too bad they don't sound like *The Lost Incas*."

"They want to be a Goth heavy-metal band," declared the rotund manager.

"Too bad they don't know how to be original."

The novelty of the first few songs wore off and people near the stage drifted away until the crowd looked like a slice of Swiss cheese.

Erin toyed with her empty glass at the bar, appearing to be a wicked temptress with sinister eyebrows and long maroon fingernails. She had slipped on a black miniskirt and squeezed into a cherry tank top to accent her curves. She saw a young prospect in a brown bomber jacket come in from the lobby and stand at the other end of the bar. He had a full face, short blonde hair, and otherwise bland features, but sparkling sapphire eyes. She leaned against the counter and asked, "Do you know him?"

"Yeah, he owns that white sports car," said the bartender. "The Fiat."

She perked up from her slouch.

Kerry had seen him too. She put something extra on the lyrics, making a song sound like a sultry ballad even though it was about teenage angst.

The guy looked away and ordered a Budweiser.

Erin possessed the passion of Olwen, a goddess who could lure any man with the hypnotic trance of her eyes. She stared in his direction until they made eye contact.

In a bold move the guy slid along the brass railing. He stopped next to her and said. "Hey, your outfit looks hot. Maybe you should be up there singing."

"Thanks." Up close, Erin had long black eyelashes which turned her eyes into mysterious dark stars. "How do you like," and her voice became soulful, "*Sunrise Beat?*"

"They're great," he said.

"On their last CD I liked the song with the fast bongo beat and searing guitar licks."

"Bongos?" Beads of sweat dotted his brow.

"The band even had steel drums and a police siren wailing on it."

"I hate to ask, but what type of music do they play?"

She breathed into his ear, "Reggae. They bring sloppiness into fashion."

"Oh, yeah, that's cool. Can I buy you a drink?"

Just then Uncle Jack slipped in between them. He demanded, "What do you want with my niece?"

"Hey, granddad, it's none of your business."

"She's not even fifteen so it is my business. And the only thing she's allowed to drink is soda water."

"You mean…?"

"Jail bait."

"I'm sorry, sir. I didn't mean to…" He slipped back to the other end of the bar.

"Oh, Uncle Jack," complained Erin. "Why do you have to ruin everything? He owned a sports car."

Tired of being teased, Montezuma slipped free of his leash in the dressing room after the show and moved toward objects like chairs, but slid by without rubbing against them. In five minutes the fiery feline had pounced on an unsuspecting mouse and seized it in between his teeth. The thin cat threatened to gobble the rodent in one bite, but instead swung it about by the scruff of its neck and dropped it. As the hapless creature attempted to scurry off, he sprung on it again, repeating the sequence many times until it was boxed in a corner.

Kerry tramped across the room and yanked on his collar, "Monty, why don't you leave that poor little thing alone?"

Montezuma remained agitated that night, prowling his home. He knocked over a trash can in the kitchen and scattered its contents, snarled at noises coming from outside, and tried to scratch up a wood chair. Kerry sang a lullaby to him, but the cat refused to calm down.

"Go get your acoustic guitar," suggested Erin.

As Kerry strummed the strings, the cat spun around and laid in his basket in the living room. She and her sister sung the lyrics to several songs alternating verses and sometimes blending their voices together. The ocelot rolled onto his back and stuck his paws in the air, drifting off to never-never land and dreaming about the tropical rain forest where he was born.

Loyal fans followed the band and its mascot, but Montezuma became sluggish on stage, ignoring commands and refusing to snarl on cue. Even when he was pushed into the darkened room with Sebastian's dog, nothing happened. They barked and snarled for a moment and then sat on opposite sides staring at each other with their luminous eyes glowing in the candlelight, weary of being bitten or scratched. The crowds gravitated to Uncle Jack, who sold bootlegged CDs of *Sunrise Beat* and *The Lost Incas*. The jam session with Nathan Honeycomb and Sebastian, recorded on someone's cell phone, became a hot selling item. A club could become empty while people gathered in the lobby and circled the display. When a prospective buyer cast a doubtful glance, Uncle Jack would say, "Let me see," and rummage through a box, "just the right item," and pull out a CD. The cover would have a photo of the lead singer of *The Lost Incas* and a title emblazoned in scarlet letters.

"Isn't it kind of expensive?" asked the customer.

"I guarantee you never heard anything like it," boasted the showman. "It was made after the guy separated from his wife and drank a bottle of tequila. Quite a unique recording session."

The poor fool would eventually stumble out of the club with empty pockets.

The band's touring took its toll on Montezuma who no longer clawed at invisible birds, but just lay in a stupor on stage. At home the cat sat on the windowsill, day after day, watching traffic go by, but nobody opened the window for fear the exhaust fumes might make him sick. The ocelot stopped to focus on one point, his eyes filled with longing. Kerry lined up behind him at that exact angle and saw a solitary, lone tree. The cat studied that tree for a solid hour.

Uncle Jack stopped by the house with an oriental gentleman who wore spectacles and a three-piece gray suit. "This is Doctor Wong," he said. "He's here to see the ocelot."

"Monty's not sick," replied Kerry. "I think he's just lonely."

"Doctor Wong is going to buy Montezuma's gall bladder for $250."

"Gall bladder very expensive," stated Doctor Wong. "We use in medicine."

"Huh?"

"And he's going to give us $200 for its liver."

"Liver too. We use. We also make jewelry from its teeth."

"You can't have him," protested Kerry.

"Throw in its pelt and paws," stated Uncle Jack, "and we're talking about over $1,000. Come on, Kerry."

"You still can't have him."

"We must take him." Uncle Jack motioned to Doctor Wong, who had put on a big pair of leather gloves to protect himself, "You swing around to the left. I'll go right."

"Run, Monty," screamed Kerry.

The cat darted under Doctor Wong's creepy reach. Kerry kicked Uncle Jack in the foot to slow him down. Then she turned over a chair to stop the doctor. She tried to stand in front of Monty, but Uncle Jack caught her from behind and wouldn't let go. The doctor cornered the cat. Kerry screamed again, "Mom...mom!"

A short, stout woman with fiery red hair dashed into the living room from the kitchen. She sized up the situation and spoke, "Put that poor animal down."

The doctor gripped the ocelot and said, "It has very nice teeth. I can make you imitation pearl earrings."

"I don't want your jewelry," seethed Kerry's mom, Doreen. "Put Montezuma down."

The doctor placed the cat on the floor, and it scurried back to its windowsill.

"What are you trying to do, Jack O'Toole? That is my daughter's pet."

He stuttered, "I...I...just thought..."

"Thought? The only thoughts you get are from the bottom of a bottle."

"Doreen, you can't blame me for taking a nip of whiskey now and then. There's a chill outside. As for the cat...I need to supplement my pension."

"I want you and the doctor to go." She pointed toward the door.

Uncle Jack looked down at the ground. His sister's daughters were the crown jewels of his life. He had been in plenty of relationships and was the subject of a half dozen paternity lawsuits. As he rambled from state to state as a sales rep, he kept one step ahead of John Law. Now he had returned home to Maryland to retire. He wanted to help Kerry and Erin in place of the kids he had left behind. He muttered, "I'm sorry, Doreen."

He and the doctor slinked out of the house.

"Kerry, he's an exotic animal," explained her mom. "We can't have him living here with us. Find him a new home."

"Aw, mom. They left."

Doreen put her hands on her hips and tilted her head. "What about the next time?"

"I'll see what I can do."

The next day Kerry and Erin visited the municipal zoo. When they entered the main office, they were surrounded by a dozen photos of animals in the wild. The zookeeper was an older gentleman who wore a tan uniform.

"This is what Montezuma looks like," said Kerry. "He's the mascot for my band, *Kerry and the Keys*." She showed him a promotional poster of the cat with his huge paws clawing the air and the band decked out in black outfits behind him.

"Oh, no!" groaned the zookeeper.

"He's not as ferocious as he looks," said Kerry. "We call him Monty."

"You want to donate him to us?"

"I think so."

"We'll have to keep him in quarantine for three weeks to monitor his health and break him of any bad habits," explained the zookeeper. "How did you get him?"

"Monty worked in a Midwest carnival," said Kerry. "Then Uncle Jack won him in a poker game with a straight flush. That's why he's been traveling with us, but he collapsed from exhaustion about a week ago. Now he spends all day gazing out our living room window."

"I'll show you where he'll end up," said the zookeeper. "Follow me."

Kerry and Erin trailed the man as he strolled outside past animal exhibits. As they climbed up a steep incline a chimpanzee chattered and charged toward them, banging off the bars of a cage. Kerry and Erin cringed. On the hilltop a bison grunted and flopped on the ground with a thud, sending a cloud of dirt floating onto their clothes. They cringed again. Finally, they hiked down a short knoll to the ocelot reserve, a space about half the size of their house. The area was shaded by a stand of poplar trees whose bare trunks poked through the wire mesh covering the cage. To one side a rock face hid the entrance of a den that could only be entered through a tiny hole, and a spring trickled from a metal pipe and formed a pool at the bottom. Another ocelot paraded back and forth on a dirt path that ran parallel to the front boundary.

"This is Lilith, the prized pet of the Amazon Queen," proclaimed the zookeeper. "We call her Lily. We obtained her from a circus stuck in Chicago because of a blizzard and an avalanche of unpaid bills. We can try to breed them. Do you still want to donate your pet?"

"I don't know," said Kerry, knowing she would be losing a friend. "What do you think, Erin?"

Erin channeled the clairvoyance of Cerridwen, who distilled from her cauldron a potion of three drops: one for the wisdom of the past, the second for knowledge in the present, and the third for the secrets of the future. She got a faraway look in her eyes and spoke, "I see them frolicking among the boulders of the rock garden and rearing a litter that will be returned to the wild. I also see something happening this weekend that will make you want to give him up."

"You do?"

"Uh-huh."

"It will be a natural reunion," stated the zookeeper. "Stop by my office next week if you decide to go through with it."

That Saturday the band had a gig scheduled in New York City. When the Amtrak train rolled out of Penn Station in Baltimore, Uncle Jack was already in a bad mood. He had lost out on the $1,000 for Montezuma and spent most of his monthly pension on rent. The girls sat together with Kerry fingering the same melody over and over again on an old acoustic guitar, trying to create a new song, and Erin reading Hollywood tabloids and spreading the gossip to anyone who would listen. Sometimes the girls giggled at nothing, sang snatches of verse together with Erin pinching her nose to sound like her favorite cartoon character, tried on different fingernail polishes that stunk up the car, or chattered about their crushes on boys. It was too much to bear so he spent most of his time in the smoking car puffing on a stogie. When they reached Grand Central Station, he shuttled them off to their hotel room while he sipped whiskey in a nearby bar. Then he roused them for the show.

With this being Montezuma's last performance, a somewhat forlorn group tramped into New York's Bitter End Nightclub while the lights were still dimmed. Kerry scanned a sea of chairs that were tossed upside down on the tables and asked, "Do you think there will be a lot of fans today?"

"What difference does it make?" stated Uncle Jack. "I've sent PR notices to 50 talent agents. Your band only has to impress them."

She galloped into the dressing room.

"Kerry's worst nightmare is playing in a place that's empty," remarked Erin. "What's yours, Uncle Jack?"

"Being down to my last keg of liquor."

Slightly red-faced and sweating, he unloaded twice as many boxes as before from the back of a cab and established the bootlegging operation in the lobby. A horde of New Yorkers descended upon him. He felt good for a while, then got a phone call. "You took the wrong train?...Where are you?...We'll make do somehow."

"What's wrong, Uncle Jack?" asked Erin.

"Sebastian got on the wrong train. He's stuck in Cleveland."

"Should we tell Kerry?"

"I'll wait until the rest of the band gets here."

Then they came. Bruce, the drummer, arrived with his wrist tucked into a cast. He had sprained it lifting weights. And Lola, with her eyes ringed with black mascara, got stage fright and stalked off. They saw her descend into the subway to spend the evening underground. Uncle Jack's bet on the Goth band was crumbling apart. His gambling jones had brought him nothing but heartache for 30 years. He went backstage and broke the bad news to his star.

Before she could cry, her sister tugged on her dress and said, "We could sing songs together like on nights when Montezuma has trouble sleeping."

"That's great," roared Uncle Jack. Then his voice tailed off, "Both of you can go on."

"I won't perform without my band!" screamed Kerry. She shook her head and peered right at him with defiant eyes.

"Come on, hon'. Everybody gets a bad break now and then."

"What do you know about it? Nothing bad ever happens to you."

"That's not true. I've been on the receiving end too," admitted Uncle Jack as he lit another stogie. "I spent a couple years in reform school. They received $500 a month from social services to house me, but were too cheap to buy a kid a lousy box of cigars."

"I'm not talking about what happened 40 years ago. I'm talking about right now!"

"Do you think it's easy for me to make ends meet?" he asked. "That's why I'm dealing T-shirts and CDs in the lobby."

"I'm sorry. I really am." Kerry looked down at the ground. "It's just so…"

"Frustrating?"

"Yeah, frustrating."

"Young lady, someday you're going to live in Hollywood and be driven around in a pink limo because…" and his tone became soft, "…you are a superstar."

The awestruck singer blushed.

A bit after 10 someone flipped on two bright spotlights and white darts shot through the black nothingness to illuminate the stage. Uncle Jack strolled forward and announced, "Tonight I present a dynamic duo from Baltimore… *The Keynotes.*"

Kerry, cradling an acoustic guitar and wearing a pretty pink dress and open-toed shoes, crept onto the platform. A touch of rouge was brushed on her cheeks and cherry gloss on her lips. Her sister, Erin, stepped forward in a navy blouse and white slacks. An orchid that shone like the pale moon was fastened in her auburn hair, showing she had become Rhiannon, ruler of the night. It was not exactly the Goth look. Kerry said, "This is a new song called *Ballad in D*" and fingered a melody.

Several patrons, expecting to hear Bruce pounding the drums and Sebastian running his hands across the keyboards, made catcalls. Uncle Jack spotted a well-dress man in a tan suit trotting toward the door. He pleaded, "Please don't leave!"

"Without Sebastian at the keys, you got nothing," he scoffed. "I wasted my time coming here." He tossed a crumbled PR notice on the floor.

Uncle Jack watched him slip out the door. He scanned the nightclub and saw that all the other guys were dressed in dark hoodies or black leather jackets. He slumped in a chair.

Meanwhile, Montezuma stalked the stage. First, he clawed at the air and tugged on his leash. Then he darted around the speakers and amplifiers. Kerry could tell by the flash of his emerald eyes he was on the hunt.

Tiny feet tickled her toes.

Montezuma snarled and leaped after his prey. His claws sunk into Kerry's shin and calf, causing blood to bead up on her skin like so many rubies.

She sung an octave higher in a soprano voice with a full vibrato, causing customers to gawk at her in amazement. Her newfound timbre came from a leg throbbing in pain. She did high-toned pirouettes while Erin dropped low into a baritone. The duet's voices were honey-coated. Bartenders stopped serving drinks while everyone turned to listen. With growing confidence, their singing became intertwined, and they shared verses together and provided background for one another on different songs. The crowd around Uncle Jack's bootlegging operation drifted into the hall.

A woman in a teal pants suit pranced up to him and inquired, "Are you their manager?"

"Yes, hon', what about it?"

"I'm Nancy Elliott with Imperial Records, LTD." She handed him her business card. He hadn't noticed her. "We're looking for new talent. Are they signed?"

Uncle Jack knew the importance of a well-placed fib, which he delivered with confidence, "We're going to Boston next week to audition for another music company. If you want to ink them, make an offer."

"Bring them to my office Monday morning, and we'll hammer out a deal. The world could always use another *Indigo Girls*."

"We'll be there."

The woman bounced back into the hall as the beautiful lyrics floated out.

Uncle Jack realized he was finally hitting the jackpot. He talked to himself, beginning with a whisper that grew louder, "They're going to become a money making machine. I'll be rich." And he twirled about like a top, leaped up onto the chair, and pushed off with a flutter in his feet.

Dust

WHEN THEY WOKE, a white vapor lingered everywhere in the forest, surrounding their cabin and flowing in-between the trees and among the taller bushes. The white blanket ranged from their homestead up into the far reaches of the hills beyond.

Thomas Hardy inhaled before speaking, "That's not fog lifting up. It smells like smog."

"All the way out here?" said Emma. "We must be 50 miles from town."

"It could be a weather inversion or some other phenomenon. Think how bad it would be if we still lived there."

Just then a park ranger in a uniform, with a firearm holstered to his belt and a cap slung over his eyes, bushwhacked through the brush. He looked up and said, "Thomas, I knew I could find you out here. A fire is rolling down the mountain. I'm ordering all the homesteaders to leave."

"A fire?" asked Thomas. "Was someone burning trash?"

"It's worse than that. Something ignited at the mine. The blaze was blowing south for a few days, then the wind changed directions."

Thomas looked at his cabin and then his wife. He planted his feet on the ground and growled, "We're not budging an inch. This is our home."

"We can't get a hotshot team out here to help you," said the ranger. "They need to protect the town from the blaze."

"We'll still not leaving."

"You don't have a firebreak," said the ranger, looking into his eyes and seeing no wavering within. "I've got some chainsaws in my ATV. I'll help you build one."

They heard the ATV's engine roaring and saw a swath of bushes being flattened as the ranger came into the clearing. He wheeled the vehicle near a line of several huge trees and stopped. They poured gasoline into the chainsaws and cranked them up. They worked in tandem, placing two V-shaped cuts in each trunk with the bottom cut determining which direction the tree fell. A line of trees came crashing down, one after another, causing sawdust to fill the air and the smell of fresh resin to be everywhere. They latched a rope around each felled tree and pulled it away from the clearing. In less than half an hour they had made a firebreak about 40 yards wide. The ranger said, "That's the best we can do. I wish you luck."

"Thanks," said Thomas, grabbing his hand in a hearty shake.

The ranger got on the ATV and rode away to warn other homesteaders. Thomas looked at his wife standing by the door and remembered their joy when their cabin was completed. She was the love of his life and he hoped the break would keep them safe. His mind drifted to the way they met when he was on the other side of the law.

• • •

A dozen protesters in rugged clothes and boots had gathered at the entrance to the strip mine, and occasionally a car or pickup would zoom by spitting up gravel from the road. Thomas Hardy showed up with his long hair pinned to his head with a red, white, and blue bandanna. A woman asked, "Are you joining our group?"

"I'm down with the protest!" he shouted.

The protesters were from Pittsburgh, Richmond, and nearby Charleston, West Virginia. They marched back and forth across the entrance carrying signs that read: "Coal = Death", "King coal brings misery", and "Ban coal". They shuffled back and forth in silence until Thomas started chanting, "We are strong; the company is wrong. Close the mine and let solar energy shine." They all joined in the chorus as though it was a church singalong.

The local sheriff got out of his car to shoo them away from the gate and wave employees into the facility. Once in a while an employee would trudge up the road from the town and gawk at them as though they were stark raving mad.

At the end of a long day, Thomas stayed with the other protesters at a makeshift camp set up in-between the coal mine and the town. They protested at the worksite for three days straight without drawing one TV or newspaper reporter. One day he was walking into town with a couple of friends. Sylvia was a dark-haired Italian beauty who had caught his eye, but she was already married to Jeff, whom she had met in college. And Jeff was a thin dude with a lot of pent-up anger who always talked about ways to "stick it to the man." Thomas stopped at a farm and leaned on a picket fence.

"Aren't you coming?" asked Sylvia.

"I want to look at the scenery for a while," he said. "Why don't you go ahead?"

"Come with us," said Jeff. "If we see a couple coal miners, we can knock their blocks off."

Thomas shrugged his shoulders.

They turned and rambled into town without him. They were used to him spacing out and looking at the landscape. It was the first time the city boy had been in the countryside.

Thomas waited until his friends were out of earshot before calling out, "People usually do that in a barn."

A young lady, who had her chestnut hair pulled into a ponytail, was sitting at a stool milking a Jersey cow. With each pull on its pink udders, the milk squirted into a pail. She replied, "Millie is skittish when I milk her inside. It used to be all right before she got spooked by a black snake."

"If you want to see a snake, you can see plenty at the coal company."

"Are you one of those out-of-towners? It used to be quiet before you all showed up."

"We're trying to save the mountain."

"Where are you from?" she asked, looking up.

"Mare-land."

"Did you say Maryland?"

"Yeah, that's what I said. Mare-land."

"The coal company provides jobs," she stated. "Folks around here need to work."

"What about the coal dust flying all over the place?" he asked. "It pollutes the water and the ground you're standing on."

"You might be right about that," she said, peering into his eyes. "When it's windy we can't put the laundry out to dry. The white linen turns gray."

"Why don't you join us?" he asked. "We could use the support of some town folks."

"The coal company has been there a long time. What's in it for me?"

"A clean environment and maybe dinner this evening."

She looked at his husky body from the toes to the shoulders and gazed at his walrus mustache, which made him look older and more distinguished. "I'll be done with my chores by six."

"You're on."

Thomas came back later that evening and took Emma to the town's diner where the locals gawked. Nevertheless, they discovered that they liked each other. She was amazed at his boldness; and he was drawn in by her simple ways and her eyes, which he thought shined as blue as a mountain lake. They kept meeting each other in town, and once in a while she would visit the protesters' camp. After a long day of tramping back and forth by the strip mine's entrance, they'd gather in the evening and sit cross-legged together in a circle. The protesters' eyes glowed as they talked about how they were changing the world.

One day the miners had dug enough coal to transport to the power plant. The protesters saw open freight cars being filled by a tall crane and decided to stop the train at the town's depot.

The miners were surprised that the protesters had dispersed from their company.

After the freight cars were filled, the locomotive pulled them down the track toward the town. It pulled into the station and had other cars coupled to the rear. The protesters came out of nowhere and gathered on the tracks in front of the train.

The conductor pulled down on the horn, and it blared.

Several protesters got scared and jumped out of the way, but Thomas Hardy stood in the middle of the tracks and held out his hand as though his palm was a stop sign. He yelled, "We will not move."

A company representative, dressed in a white shirt and dark tie, stood on the depot's platform and screamed, "Run them over."

The train's horn blared again.

Still Thomas did not move. The other protesters cowered behind him, with one foot on the railroad bed ready to jump off.

The rep yelled again, "Run them over!"

A window to the locomotive screeched open and the train conductor poked his head out, his brow furrowed. "I can't do it."

It took half an hour for the state police to arrive. They arrested the protesters one by one with Thomas being the last to be dragged away. As they were loaded into a paddy wagon, the train rolled out of the station. Coal ash spilled off several cars, filling the air and making them cough and sneeze. They watched as the train rolled into the distance, its horn wailing in triumph.

The protesters' actions created a buzz around town. Some people wondered whether there was a serious problem with strip mining while others couldn't understand why the police couldn't force the outsiders to leave. Consequently, the mayor decided to hold a public hearing to resolve the issues. It was scheduled on a Wednesday evening and most of the town's residents attended. Several protesters stood before the assembled crowd and presented graphs and charts about the pollution caused by mining and transporting coal. They prattled on about parts per million and EPA standards. Meanwhile, a representative of the company talked about how they used best practices in mining coal, reclaimed strip-mined land, and provided more jobs to the town's citizens than any other employer.

Then Mary Canterbury tottered up to the podium. She was an elderly lady with a pompadour of gray hair and wrinkles fanning out from her eyes and mouth.

"She's always complaining about something," quipped someone in the crowd.

Mary plunked a mason jar on the podium and said, "The mine is fouling my well water." The water in the jar was clear at the top, yellowish in the middle, and had a black film on the bottom.

"It doesn't look that bad," stated the mayor.

Thomas Hardy bounced up to the podium, causing gasps to come from the crowd, grabbed the jar, and shook it up and down. When he plunked it back on the podium, black dust was suspended in the water. He roared, "That's what it looks like when it comes out of her well. Would you drink that?"

"Well, um..." The mayor was stumped.

"That's not a problem," said the company representative. "We can provide her with bottled water."

"It's not the same," sneered Mary, who stomped back to her seat.

The town council convened for about 15 minutes and voted 6 to 1 not to restrict any mining operations. Residents who were employed at the mine nodded their agreement with the decision while Mary Canterbury grumbled to anyone seated nearby. The protesters sagged in their seats with disappointment as everyone left the meeting hall.

Thomas and the others trudged to their campsite and began tearing it down because "changing the world" would have to wait. Some hitchhiked out of town on Main Street; others gathered at the bus station, which was across the street from a tavern.

Thomas saw the mayor, council president, and the company representative get out of their cars, crack a few jokes, and pat each other on the back. They entered the tavern to get a brew as though they were old friends. He sat on a bench, shaking his head.

Emma came down the street and found him there. She asked, "Are you going away?"

"I was thinking about getting a piece of land and settling down if I could find someone to share it with."

"And...?"

"Would you?"

"Of course," she gushed, hugging him.

They were married by Emma's father, who was a deacon in the local church. Her relatives were not sure what to make of this strange man who rarely smiled and didn't know how to clog to the tunes of the jug band that performed at their reception. But Emma grinned from ear to ear, and her happiness was all that counted.

The couple found a secluded cabin in the nearby Allegheny Mountains that they obtained from the park service in exchange for maintenance and other work. During the spring and fall, they counted migratory birds; and during the other months, they tracked an occasional black bear or mountain lion that had ravaged a camp site. Thomas chopped the firewood and learned how to hunt. Emma tended a garden and milked several goats kept in a pen. Both of them cooked on a wood stove; and Emma baked bread, cakes, and pies.

They lived off the grid without a television or radio, but their evenings were not quiet. Emma could play a fiddle and Thomas learned how to pluck a banjo and sing lyrics to bluegrass songs.

Thomas recalled the last time someone visited. He was spreading feed out to his chickens when he heard boots stomping through the bushes. When Jeff burst into the clearing, he yelled, "Brother, how'd you find us?"

"I knew you were out here somewhere," said Jeff, looking behind himself in both directions.

"Did you bring someone with you?" asked Thomas, gazing into the bushes.

"I want to make sure no police followed me."

"Out here?" said Thomas. "It's just us."

"Why don't you come inside?" said Emma. "I'll get you some tea and something to eat."

They gathered around a table by the wood stove. Emma began brewing tea and placed what remained of a peach cobbler in front of them. She had been craving fruit pies lately and had become a bit bloated.

"Jeff, what are you doing out here?" asked Thomas.

"I've got a plan to get back at the coal company and teach them a lesson."

"What's your plan?" asked Emma, cutting slices from the cobbler.

Jeff looked around inside the cabin before he whispered, "We can sneak in there after midnight. There's only one guard then. I'll pour gasoline over the backhoes while you keep watch. We'll set the blaze and split."

Emma set out cups of tea for all of them and sat down. She had a puzzled look on her face. "Why would we want to do that?"

"To get back at them!" shouted Jeff, banging his fist on the table. "To stop them from taking off the mountaintop."

"We don't think it makes any difference," said Thomas.

"What do you mean?" asked Jeff, contorting his face into a strange shape.

"We don't think it makes any difference what we do, what you do, or what anyone does. The politicians will party until the planet is dead.

That's why we're living here...to get a slice of something before it's all gone."

"Why don't you settle down?" added Emma. "You and Sylvia could get a place of your own and be happy for a while. It doesn't have to be out here in the wilderness."

They shared the peach cobbler and tea with him. Jeff became calm and lounged with them for about an hour. When he left, they were sure he had forgotten about his bizarre scheme.

• • •

Now there appeared to be two suns shining in the sky, one from the west and the other from the east. A plume of smoke darkened the sky. Embers floated about like fireflies, lighting up the air all around them; and wherever they landed, on a tree branch or bush, a fire flared up, crackling the wood with combustion. They saw the blaze come up over the ridge. The flames leaped 50 feet high.

"I'm not worried about myself," said Emma, peering into his eyes, "but I'm pregnant. I don't want my baby to die."

"We'll pack supplies and go down to the river."

They released their chickens and goats, which scattered in different directions. Then they scurried around the cabin stuffing food and clothes into two knapsacks. By the time they got outside the roof had caught fire.

"Come on," said Thomas. "Run!"

They trotted down the trail carrying a shovel in one hand and lugging the packs. Fires flared up all around them and flames danced on tree branches. Black smoke wafted in the air, irritating their eyes and making them cover their noses and mouths with handkerchiefs so they could breathe. The river was still a quarter mile away and the heat was as intense as a day in midsummer in the midafternoon.

Thomas stopped, dropped his knapsack, and said, "Leave the supplies behind."

Emma dropped her knapsack.

They both hustled along the trail again. After they had gone about a dozen yards, he heard Emma yelp, "Thomas."

He spun around and saw her sprawled on the ground.

"I've turned my ankle." A look of desperation was etched on her face.

"Give me the shovel." He kneeled down and said, "Hold onto me."

She clambered onto his back and wrapped her arms around his neck and chest.

Thomas lifted her up, holding a shovel in each hand. He hiked down the trail huffing with each step. Any ordinary man would have collapsed from the weight he was carrying, but his limbs were strong from working in the forest every day. When he got to the stream, most of the water had already evaporated. It usually ran five or six feet deep, but there was only about a foot or two left in the center of a gully.

He dropped Emma down and said, "We'll dig a trench in the mud and cover ourselves up."

The trees had caught fire on both sides of the bank, and the heat was becoming unbearable. Emma stared at the blaze in a bewildered way.

"Don't look at the flames," he screamed. "Dig!"

She plopped on her knees and started digging. He dug the shovel in too, digging a trench for her. Branches were crackling with fire and exploding apart, sounding like firecrackers and spewing embers everywhere. The trench they dug for her was only a foot deep. She laid down in it and he covered her up with mud.

He felt as though he was baking in an oven. The air was thin, being consumed by the fire, making him wheeze. He plopped to his knees and dug in with a shovel. He felt a shearing pain on his back and smelled smoke coming off of him. He peeled off his shirt, which exploded in flames, and tossed it onto the bank.

He had run out of time, and the trench would only cover half his body. He saw a little pool of water left. He fell into the puddle and coated his upper body and head with clumps of mud. He trudged back to the trench and placed his legs and waist in it. He packed mud on top of his lower body, laid face down, and covered his head with his mud-caked arms.

They had buried themselves like two frogs in the mud. The fire roared down into the canyon, sounding like a freight train rolling down the tracks at top speed. Tree trunks exploded apart and the earth became heated from the flames. It felt as though he was buried on a beach baking underneath the sand. He dared not move a limb or be scorched. He had trouble catching his breath as the fire sucked all the air out of the river basin. He lay sprawled in the mud exhausted and gasping for air.

After the fire had roared by, Thomas heard the occasional popping of a smoldering ember. He pushed himself up to his knees with the dried mud cracking apart. Standing up, he felt dazed. He stomped his feet and shook his arms to get the blood flowing, feeling pins and needles all over his body. A thought flashed in his mind.

"Emma," he screamed. She was still buried alive in the mud.

He plopped to his knees and clawed at the ground, tearing at the small round air hole. Clumps of clay broke apart in his hands and the hole widened.

"I can't breathe," he heard her whimper.

"I'm digging you out," he yelled. He grabbed a pointed rock nearby and raked the ground above her. While wisps of smoke wafted by, he dug. Finally, there was enough loose soil to pull her out.

She sat up, still buried from the waist down, and gasped for air. She began clawing at the ground.

He kneeled by her buried feet and dug.

After a few minutes, enough of the soil above her was loose. He helped her to her feet. He wanted to sponge the dirt from her body, but all the water in the river had evaporated.

They trudged along the dry riverbed. They saw the blackened remains of a wood lodge and a beaver sprawled out 10 yards away. Though its body was not burned, it was dead nonetheless, suffocated when the fire sucked the air out of the gully. He turned around and gazed at the place where they had buried themselves. A lip of the riverbank had curled overtop them, preserving a pocket of air. He had chosen the spot at random, and serendipity had saved them.

They found the trail and started hiking back to their home. Only charred stalagmites marked where the forest had been. They saw the singed remains of squirrels, opossums, and raccoons that could not outrun the blaze. They occasionally stopped and swiveled their heads, seeing a barren landscape in their valley. Each footstep sounded drearier than the one before. When they came upon their clearing, they saw that the cabin had been burned down to its stone foundation. Only one charred pillar stood by the missing door.

"We're okay, Thomas," said Emma, holding her belly. "That's all that counts."

"Are you really pregnant?"

"Yes."

He came over and hugged her from behind. He looked down at her belly and said, "That's good. You're both safe."

"I figure if it's a boy, we'll call him Jude," she said. "If it's a girl, let's call her Tess."

"I like that name…Tess."

Thomas Hardy plodded over to the cabin and touched the pillar. It crumbled to dust.

Neptune's Garden

It was a picture-perfect day with the temperature in the 70s, an azure-blue sky, and a gentle breeze causing ripples to lap against the rooftop pool's edge when a man stepped in front of me and muttered, "Mr. Barrett, I am here on behalf of Consolidated Seed. May I talk to you."

I wondered what this punk thought was going on. Hoshi, my girlfriend, had let him into the penthouse suite when he asked to see me. He appeared to be in his early twenties with chubby cheeks and soft hands, and looked uncomfortable in a pinstriped suit with beads of sweat popping up on his brow. He had probably never been out of the office before. I snapped, "What do you want?"

The punk took out a sheet of paper and spoke, "Consolidated Seed has invested funds in an aquatic garden on Georges Bank, off of Cape Cod. A few days ago someone sabotaged the project. They are offering you $50,000 to conduct an investigation."

There were at least 1,000 private dicks that Consolidated Seed could ask to investigate their case, but they came to me. I gazed across the street at the Gold Dust Casino's neon sign and thought about all the fools who lost a fortune at the gambling tables. Consolidated Seed might be afraid of losing a significant amount of money on this venture so I decided to call their bluff. "I'll accept the case for $150,000 plus expenses. Half up front and the other half when I wrap up my investigation."

"Mr. Barrett, they're only offering $50,000," stammered the punk, whose hand started shaking. He looked about the pool and back at me. He rolled his hand as if expecting something more from me; then realizing nothing was going to happen, pulled out his cell phone and dialed his boss. "He's asking for $150,000 plus expenses. I don't know how long he thinks it will take…Mr. Barrett, how long do you think the investigation will take?"

I didn't say a thing. I was upset that this punk was blocking the sunlight and ruining an otherwise pleasant day. He could get the hell out for all I cared.

The punk kept looking at his phone and me, waiting for someone to speak. "He's not saying anything. Mr. Barrett, would you consider $100,000?" Once again his eyes darted back and forth from his phone to me, still expecting an answer that didn't come. Then he listened to someone on the other end of the phone. "Yes, sir. I'll tell him."

He pocketed the phone and became stone cold when he spoke, "They'll give you the $150,000 plus expenses."

That afternoon I let Hoshi give my back a good rub with her nimble hands before we had sex. I could go out with any of the women who worked at the Gold Dust Casino, but I chose her because she was adorable with a petite body, cute face, silky black hair, and ebony eyes. Plus, those Japanese women know how to take care of their men. I sent her away later that afternoon to begin the case.

Reed McIntosh, a diving instructor, looked like a tugboat captain with his sunburnt skin and burly chest. We slipped on wet suits and strapped on tanks of compressed air. I adjusted the mask covering my eyes and nose before plunging into the deep end of the pool. Although I had been snorkeling before in the Caribbean, diving proved to be more complex. I had to learn new swim strokes for underwater movement and several methods of coming up to the surface in staged decompressions. At one point, I scraped the cement bottom and the regulator was ripped out of my mouth, making me leap out of the water and cough water out of my lungs. We went through a dozen tanks of air by sunset.

"We've been at this all day," stated Reed. "Are you going on a salvage operation?"

"No, I'm conducting an investigation on Georges Bank."

"Georges Bank? That's deep diving. You could get nitrogen narcosis or a case of the bends."

I shrugged my shoulders.

• • •

At five the next morning I caught a flight from Atlantic City to Boston's Logan International Airport. I took a helicopter to an office building downtown, landed on the roof, and rode the elevator down to our makeshift office on the 11th floor. When I opened the door, Tabitha, my assistant, was sitting at a computer console with her fingers dancing across the keyboard. She's an African-American woman with straight light-brown hair falling down to her neck.

"Rick, it's good to see you," she said over her shoulder. "I've contacted Consolidated Seed. You'll need four security clearances to work with the scientific database at the undersea station. I'm putting in the paperwork right now."

I moseyed up behind her and massaged her shoulders. "It's good to see you too. Real good."

"Rick, don't you think about anything else? We got a case to work on."

I kissed her neck and murmured, "I'm sure we can find time for that later."

"My boyfriend owns a Smith & Wesson."

"You've got a point there."

She had always stuck to business ever since I hired her. I met her while she was suspended from the NYPD for getting too rough with a suspect. I comforted her and gave her a sympathetic ear. After I slept with her, she was open to a lot of suggestions. She was tired of being hounded by the Internal Affairs Unit and eager to move on. Now I give her a 25% cut to set up an office wherever I need to work and provide 24/7 assistance, which isn't bad on most cases, since I usually wrap them up in two to three weeks.

"How bad is the sabotage?" I asked her while the security pass was printing out.

"A Dr. Lassiter may have been murdered. He was working on Project Neptune."

"It sounds like a bit more than sabotage. What does the police report say?"

She wheeled around and looked at me with those mahogany eyes. "They have two problems: jurisdiction and evidence."

"The undersea station is too far away for anyone to claim jurisdiction?"

73

"That's right."

"And the evidence?"

Her countenance became grim. "A coworker saw a cloud of blood in the water and the tail of a great white shark swimming away. When he got nearer, he realized that Lassiter's upper body was wedged into a mechanical door. His skull and left arm had been crushed. The rest of his body hasn't been recovered yet."

"How soon can I get out there?"

"The supply sub won't leave port until tomorrow, but we can put you on the deck of the U.S.S. Benjamin Franklin in two hours. They're patrolling the perimeter of the project space."

The helicopter lifted off with a whop…whop…whop…and I headed out to sea past the docks with cranes unloading cargo, tugs hauling freighters into port, sailboats skipping just offshore, and a fishing fleet farther out. We flew 2,000 feet up with the Atlantic's blue floor below us, and everywhere I looked there was nothing in sight but blinding sunlight coming down from above and being reflected from the water's surface. We kept going for another 20 minutes, then spotted a speck of gray below. The pilot descended and slowed down. We had traveled 90 miles offshore to the edge of the Continental Shelf, which was hidden under the ocean.

A sliver of silver sliced through the seawater. The U.S.S. Benjamin Franklin was an Arleigh Burke-class guided missile destroyer, 500 feet long and displacing 9,000 tons. Rows of torpedo tubes and a gun turret were in the bow and missile batteries aligned the deck. The helicopter flew over the masts, which no longer held sails but rather advanced radar and communications systems. When we landed on a platform in the stern, a flight crew came out and fastened the helicopter down. I stepped off the rotary-winged aircraft and gained my sea legs, smelling salt and diesel fuel in the air.

I was led to the command center in the bridge, which overlooked the armaments in the bow and had a clear view of the ocean ahead of us. The commander was a stump of a man, 5'6", thick in the waist and chest. He waddled back and forth on the bridge. "Barrett…Richard Barrett? I've heard of your exploits in Libya."

"I travel all over the world…if the money is right."

The commander stopped and stared at me. He proclaimed, "We do it for love of country."

"Don't you get tired of having your ear bent to what the pentagon says?"

"We take our orders direct from the President. There are U.S. citizens down there and our duty is to protect them."

"All I see is ocean?"

"It's what's underneath the surface." He began to waddle back and forth again, but this time he was in deep thought as if trying to solve a puzzle. "We've been tracking a Russian sub for the last two weeks."

"Are they monitoring what's going on at the undersea station?"

"Your guess is as good as mine. They'll tip their hand sooner or later." He clasped his palms together. "So much for the chitchat. Let me show you around this old catcher."

We toured the gun turret and missile batteries in the bow and walked around to the port side. I saw a reddish-brown spot, about a half mile wide, out on the ocean, probably an oil slick or spent diesel fuel discharged from the Russian sub. The commander's reaction was to show me the squid mortar that could lob a projectile 250 yards and then have it sink to a depth of 150 to 1,000 feet before detonating.

Shrill bells rang out all over the ship three times in a row. An officer marched up to the commander and saluted.

"Yes, ensign?"

"Our underwater drone has detected an incursion on the northern perimeter."

"Assemble the team."

"Yes, sir."

"Barrett, this is your chance to get a firsthand look at what's going on."

Both of us donned the dark blue wetsuits of the Navy, got tanks of compressed air, and received spear guns from the armory. We gathered in several speed boats with two dozen Navy SEALs. As the boats hydroplaned across the water in the opposite direction of the U.S.S. Benjamin Franklin, the commander explained, "The Russian sub will pick up our destroyer going west. We'll drop in behind them and catch them by surprise."

The speed boats traveled about five miles and then the boatswains turned off the engines, allowing us to skim across the surface in silence. We came to a spot of the right latitude and longitude and the boatswains brought us to a stop.

The commander was the first one to plunge into the water. I followed with the rest of the team. We spread out about 10 yards apart and descended. The water was crystal clear for a spell then became darker as the ambient sunlight faded. We swam through the seawater with schools of silvery-blue fish dispersing in front of us.

Then I saw what we were swimming toward: a field of seaweed on a plateau that was elevated above the murky water below. The penetration of sunlight had diminished, making everything visible as though through a misty fog. The fronds of the plants, which stood three times taller than rows of corn, were a brilliant green and twisted and turned with the flow of water. I saw Russian aquanauts in scarlet wetsuits coming in and out of the field and about a half dozen of them gathered around a treasure chest like the petals of a rose.

We were descending from above and from a different direction than they expected. The two dozen Navy frogmen were now spread out in a drag net.

One Russian turned around and straightened up, spotting us.

Before he could warn the others, spears sizzled through the water, striking him in the shoulder and stomach. He crumbled over.

"What!?" my mind screamed as the Navy SEALs and I closed the trap.

Other Russian aquanauts in their scarlet wetsuits straightened up and spun around, looking like a formidable platoon.

Spears sizzled in both directions. The diver beside me got struck and sunk toward the bottom. I swam into battle not knowing why we fought.

Two Russian aquanauts grabbed the treasure chest and took off. Several others stood their ground to provide protective fire.

Most of the Navy SEALs peeled off to go after the treasure chest. I stayed on the left flank of our line. I saw a flash of scarlet in the water.

A Russian aquanaut was swimming away from me. Then I saw three more of them flutter-kicking away.

When I glanced to either side, I did not see anyone from the Navy SEALs. I thought it was strange that even though the odds were in their favor, four to one, they turned and swam. I stopped and spun around.

Then I saw it: a great white shark over 20 feet in length and weighing close to 2,000 pounds, which was propelling itself by swinging its tail from side to side. Because it was above me I didn't notice its bluish-gray dorsal and pectoral fins, but only that huge white underbelly. It was diving down toward me.

I raised my spear gun and squeezed the trigger.

The great white veered to the right and the spear scooted by without even nicking it. The shark swam at over 30 miles an hour.

I spun around as it slid by. It did not swim away, but came back toward me in a wide arc. I fumbled with the extra spear. When I looked up, all I could see was its gaping mouth and rows of razor-sharp, serrated teeth. I held the spear gun with one hand and pulled out my knife with the other.

If I panicked, there would be no tomorrow. I looked down its gaping mouth and waved my hands as it came upon me. The spear gun was knocked out of my hand and the knife missed its body, which then slithered away.

I dove straight down and swam for the rocks, looking for the spear gun. The glint of steel flashed a few yards away. I propelled myself with powerful flutter kicks, knowing my life hung in the balance. I snatched the gun from the soft sand and loaded the extra spear without looking for the great white. I knew it would be coming for me from another direction. A school of cod was hiding among the rocks, but I was too big to disappear among them. I spun around to the direction I thought the great white would be coming from. Sometimes you got to roll the dice. I was right.

Its teeth gleamed underwater and its tail wagged, propelling its huge body toward me once again. The closer it came, the more its teeth seemed like daggers.

I had one shot to hit the mark. If I missed my target, it would be over. My first shot went wide. The second one might too. I lowered the spear gun until it was parallel to me. I calculated that I had only one bet to place. I pulled the trigger.

The spear went underneath the belly of the shark.

I dove deeper until I was hugging the bottom, hoping that my bet would pay off.

The great white swam overtop me and circled around. When it came back, it swam farther up in the water toward a puff of blood. My spear had hit one of the cods. The shark's teeth tore off a piece of the cod's flesh. A hundred pounds of fish would keep it busy for a while. I swam along the bottom of the seafloor and up a slope toward the field of seaweed.

I found the Navy frogmen gathering on the other side of the green fronds. Some of them crumbled over from being hit by spears; others carried Russian aquanauts that had been hit or captured. We floated up toward the surface, stopping every 30 feet in a staged decompression. When we reached the speed boats, I clambered aboard one and helped the wounded Navy SEALs aboard. The boatswains raced back to the destroyer to get to the medic as soon as possible.

The U.S.S. Benjamin Franklin had a cargo net draped over its starboard side. I watched as several Navy SEALs scrambled up the net onto the deck and dropped stretchers for the wounded. I tightened a tourniquet around one Navy SEAL's leg and helped to load him on a stretcher. Finally, I climbed up the cargo net to the deck.

Boarding the vessel, I saw divers dragging their scuba gear back to their quarters and several bodies sprawled out on the deck. The masks had been taken off the Russian aquanauts to reveal vacant eyes staring at the sky and faces contorted into grim forms. There were holes torn in their scuba suits by the spears, which had been pulled out of their flesh.

I dropped off my scuba gear and made my way to the command center in the bridge. The commander was checking on the location of the Russian sub when I entered. When he saw me, I asked, "What's going on down there?"

"We sent the Russians a message that there is a cost to jeopardizing the safety of U.S. citizens at the undersea station," said the commander, "and in trying to steal government secrets."

An ensign came into the office and said, "Seaman Johnson has bled out."

"Send a message to his family in Erie that he died in a training accident."

"Yes, sir." The ensign spun around and left the office.

"There is a cost to both sides," said the commander. "Seaman Johnson was so eager to serve his country, but he found out we are not kids spurring in a schoolyard."

A petty officer came up to the bridge lugging a black dry bag and said, "We found what they were after."

He opened the bag and laid out several strips of kelp that had been cut from the garden under the sea. Then he took photos of the specimens and jotted down information in a written report.

The commander stated, "Our job is to document the incursion and report it to the undersea station and the Pentagon."

"All of this fighting over a bag of kelp?"

"Barrett, we have come a long way from a thousand years ago," explained the commander. "Back then the Vikings fished off the Grand Banks of Newfoundland. They were the only people around. Now you have over a hundred nations who want to claim the resources under the oceans."

"You guys are killing each other," I said. "It's an undeclared war."

The commander chuckled at my ignorance. He said, "The civil wars in the Sudan and Syria erupted after famines. In the near future there will be 10 billion people on the planet. Every acre of arable land will already be claimed for agriculture. Society will have to look at the acres on the seafloor. Right now nations are jockeying in the Arctic Ocean to exploit the minerals under the ice. China is building artificial islands in the South Pacific and claiming dominion over the resources nearby. The next world war might occur because of the superpowers clashing over the possession of the oceans."

• • •

Around noon the next day a sub ferrying supplies to the research station pulled alongside the destroyer. I clambered aboard, my feet ringing against its shell, and dropped into its belly. I was led to the operations center where I stayed for the journey. All the hatches were shut and shrill bells rung. The vessels pulled apart, and the sub was swallowed up by the immense ocean. As it dived, the color of the water changed from clear to light blue. The sub cruised over a canyon ridge and dove deeper still with the water turning a royal blue. Then I saw an array of white lights illuminating the outline of the station, which was composed of two dozen octagonal-shaped units sunk into the sand on steel stilts. The sub slowed down and docked. Through the porthole I saw a pod of brown tiger sharks swimming along the bottom, making me realize that danger lurked everywhere. An air lock formed in-between the sub and undersea station. I stepped through the connected doorway.

I walked down a hallway to the administrator's office, whose walls were full of diplomas and certificates because wherever I looked there were three or four walls forming angles instead of two. Dr. Winston, an older man with a gray goatee, sat behind a stainless steel desk and spoke with an aura of distinction, "A lot of things may appear strange to you; but if you stay long enough, you'll understand."

"From what I know this undersea station has been in operation for two years," I said. "Can you tell me about it?"

Dr. Winston leaned back in his chair and interlocked the fingers of both hands before saying, "We are proof that an oasis can be created in the middle of the ocean. This station is a scientific storehouse where experiments can be conducted and new products tested. Already, we are responsible for the development of fourteen biotech patents. And everything came from a humble beginning."

I leaned closer and urged him, "Go on."

"The first SDC, submersible decompression chamber, was built in the last century at Great Stirrup Cay in the Bahamas," he said. "Two aquanauts spent 48 hours at a depth of 70 fathoms exploring the ocean bottom. From that beginning over 50 years ago we have come to this…a cradle for an underwater civilization. Right now architects are drawing up plans for a city of 10,000 inhabitants. If we tap into the geothermal energy along the Atlantic Rift, we can become self-sufficient."

I decided to throw him another softball question. "What type of work do the scientists do?"

"The scientists here…"

Just then a slinky looking babe with long, soft auburn hair popped into the office. Her tanned thighs were capped off by a cherry-red miniskirt and white blouse.

"This is one of them.... Dr. Patricia Conway. She'll be your liaison. And this is...."

"Richard Barrett." I shook her limp hand.

"I'm Trish. I'm real pleased to meet you." She smiled as she sat in the chair next to mine and her green eyes glistened. "I hope Jeremy hasn't been boring you."

"No, not at all."

"Ah-umm...The scientists here are involved in all phases of the cultivation of marine plants and fish species. We have lab facilities for 10 scientific teams and a supporting crew of 18. For specific projects you will need to talk directly to the scientists involved."

"And the funding?"

"We receive funding from Consolidated Seed, of course, but we also rely on grants from the government."

I decided to zero in on the bulls'-eye. "What about Dr. Lassiter's project?"

He gasped, finally realizing why I was there. Regaining his composure, he said, "Dr. Lassiter's work did generate a lot of scientific curiosity and additional funding."

"What he's not saying, Barrett, is that most people have a head-in-the-sand approach to the future," interrupted Trish. "Dr. Lassiter was light-years ahead of his time. Most scientists just duplicate tests that have already been done, but Paul was more than a fact checker. He knew how to speculate."

"And that speculation got him killed?"

Trish winced. "Maybe."

I peered at Dr. Winston, who looked like a stooge who had just lost his bet at the blackjack table unable to realize that the dealer's two hands were more often better than his one.

"It could have been an accident," said Dr. Winston. "Nitrogen narcosis."

"Nitrogen narcosis?"

"Nitrogen narcosis occurs when too much nitrogen has been forced into the diver's body because of increased water pressure. It causes slower reaction time and hallucinations. That day they worked at depths of 50 to 60 fathoms. Dr. Lassiter could have had a delayed reaction."

"Have there been other accidents?"

"Three in the last year."

"Three divers?"

Dr. Winston was breathing heavy, seeing his future funding slipping away. "Three pairs of divers. Six people. Usually nitrogen narcosis has to affect both divers for them to lose control. If it only affects one diver, the other can help."

"And Dr. Lassiter?"

"You need to talk to Jody."

Jody, who was as tall as a giant, had a dark beard that covered his face and big, brooding eyes. If he was the killer, it would take a dozen men to subdue him. He was Dr. Lassiter's assistant since the project began, and they developed three plots of kelp: two near the station and one in the blue euphotic zone. Their task was to strengthen aquatic plants by giving them the genes of other plants, for example, corn. They wanted to breed a strain that could grow where other aquatic plants couldn't. Then they could plant and till an area the size of Iowa, creating an undersea breadbasket.

"Can you tell me about the accident?" I asked.

"Dr. Lassiter and I had just come back from the blue euphotic zone using turbine sleds. Dr. Lassiter was putting the sweeper into the storage shed."

"What does a sweeper do?"

"The sweeper is a vacuuming tool that clears the sea bottom before planting."

"Okay. Where were you while Dr. Lassiter was at the shed?"

"I went to put our samples into the containment bin. I returned to the shed about 10 minutes later."

I leaned forward. "Why did it take you so long?"

"I was watching a manta ray flapping its wings like an underwater butterfly. I am still fascinated…"

"A manta ray?" I barked.

"…by the ocean. Yes, a manta ray."

Jody told me how he came back and found the bloody remains of Dr. Lassiter. The whole time he was talking I wondered what type of fool he took me for - thinking that a big guy like him behaved like a child. Experience taught me to keep my cool, and that's what I did.

That night I was shown to the visitor center, a condensed quarters barely big enough for two bunk beds and a card table. On the wall there was a diagram of the station which showed two docking areas and five lockout chambers for divers. In that place, all alone, I felt the ocean currents wrapping around the outer shell and squeezing tight. I peered out a porthole into pitch-black darkness and wondered if the station might someday be crushed like a tin can. As a child my parents had to drag me to the community pool for lessons. And there I was at the bottom of the biggest swimming pool on the East Coast, the Atlantic Ocean.

• • •

Early the next morning I walked into a lab with the sea's slimy creatures - eels, sea urchins, and jellyfish - stuffed into bins on top of a work table. Trish was dissecting a four-inch long fish.

"This is the worst part," she said, "washing them down and dividing them into slides. Using biological equations we can map their growth rates with a computer simulated model, but it's not the same as the real thing. Give me another minute."

I straddled a stool, content to watch her.

She wiped her hands on a towel.

I noticed a constellation of freckles scattered on her cheeks and her cat-like green eyes. I pointed toward the other items and asked, "What about them?"

"We study the metabolism rates of different organisms for zooplankton. Zooplankton is the most abundant microorganism in the ocean. All fingerlings survive on them."

"How'd you get into this?"

"When I was a little girl, we trapped mud cats in puddles along the Tombigbee river," she said, leaning against the table and looking small. "I grew up and began to study them in school. Over 2,000 different species. Catfish, catfish, catfish. People don't know it, but most of the fish they eat - bass, perch, catfish - are all grown in commercial ponds on farms. Two pounds of feed produce one pound of fish. Fifteen pounds, for beef cattle."

"So you help corporations make box lunches for consumers except for the hush puppies and Cole slaw."

"I suppose. I've moved on to another designer fish since then: Atlantic salmon. We're using a flounder's gene to develop a breed that can survive in temperatures as low as 29 degrees Fahrenheit; thereby extending its range. Then we can raise them in pens on the bottom of the Grand Banks off Newfoundland."

"How does that connect to Dr. Lassiter's project?"

"It doesn't. The only thing I can tell you about Paul is that he had an intense rivalry with Dr. Raymond. They both worked in the same field."

"Did they have any disagreements?"

"Some researchers believed that Paul rushed his experiments into field tests. Dr. Raymond was one of them. I heard them arguing once in the cafeteria. Paul was also subject to a lawsuit by the Free Oceans Network. They were trying to shut him down."

"What happened to the lawsuit?"

"It's still pending."

"And the disagreement with Dr. Raymond?"

"In my own experiments, I've spent the last two years checking the susceptibility of salmon offspring to diseases and parasites, reconfirming growth rates, and going over everything to the nth degree." She paused, her face shining with inner radiance. "But Paul didn't need to do all that double-checking. He considered himself a genius."

After Trish's assistant took over in the lab, we strolled to lockout chamber # 2. I put on an orange wetsuit, and she slipped into one that was flamingo-pink. The chamber began to fill with water. During the 20 minutes it took to pressurize the water to the outside depth we checked our tanks and regulators. Divers at the undersea station practiced closed-circuit diving where the diver's exhaled air was recirculated in a closed loop back through a carbon dioxide scrubber and reused again, resulting in no air bubbles. That made anyone at the undersea station virtually invisible in the seawater and therefore a suspect. It was similar to placing a bet on the roulette wheel which had so many different outcomes, any number could hit. After the pressure was aligned, Trish opened the hatch and swam out.

I followed her, noticing how the colors were muted by the lack of sunlight in the water. Her wetsuit appeared to be crimson while mine turned brown. The bottom of the undersea station was encrusted with a layer of barnacles and sponges. A school of fish darted around a steel leg. The ocean floor was covered with jagged rocks, shells, scattered clumps of seaweed, anemones, and green reefs made up of algae and sponges, tube worms, and crustaceans. Visibility was limited to 100 feet. After that everything dissolved into cloudy darkness.

The air I breathed felt heavy in my lungs, causing me to became sluggish and slow down. I stopped. I began to float back weightless in the current with my arms and legs dangling like a starfish.

Trish swam back toward me, looking like a fiery demonic messenger in her crimson wetsuit. For a moment I flashed back to a childhood nightmare with fear shooting up my spine as the devil, himself, came upon me. Even the incantations of a catholic priest, suspended in midair or midwater, could not stop him. With concentrated effort I lowered my right arm to belt level and grabbed the round handle of my serrated knife.

The crimson demon yanked my mouthpiece away from me.

I straightened up and slid the knife out of its sleeve. Then I peered at the emerald eyes shining behind the demon's mask and realized it was only the gaze of a woman. I got a grip on myself.

Trish tasted the air I was breathing and adjusted the helium intake on the hose. She tasted it again. She put my mouthpiece back in and gave me a thumbs up.

Within a minute a surge of strength flowed into my limbs. I shook the cobwebs out of my head and swam after her again. We were going to tour the storage shed and fish pens.

I examined the automatic door to the storage shed which was operated by the divers from an outside control panel. Its sound was muted by the whining engine of a fish trawler a couple of miles away. The acreage around the station was off limits to fishing and marked off by buoys.

Meanwhile, Trish danced like a ballerina from one fish pen to the next, taking notes on a handheld computer. The pens, which were enclosed by Plexiglas panels, contained fish separated by size.

I measured the distance and time it took to swim from the storage shed to the containment bins and back: three minutes to cover 140 yards.

Trish signaled that she was ready to go back.

I swam behind her to the lockout chamber. It took several minutes for the seawater to be pumped back out.

"These little buggers are getting big," yelped Trish, holding a container of fingerlings. "I adjusted your intake valve to nine percent helium. For deeper dives go up to 30 percent. It takes time getting used to tri-mix."

For divers tri-mix was a blend of oxygen, nitrogen, and helium used to prevent them from getting oxygen toxicity and other ailments. Even though I had no experience with it, I said, "I must go down deeper to the blue euphotic zone."

"You'll have to see Jody about that."

We placed our tanks in the corner. She opened a box against the wall and pulled out a set of towels.

"When we were teenagers, we would race around this curve on the road by the river. If you went far enough onto the shoulder, you could really spray gravel." She laughed nervously. "Then, one evening my friends, Nicky and Greg, went over the embankment and drowned in their car."

"I joined the army's special forces unit to do things no none else could do like parachuting out of a plane at midnight," I said. "I learned that what separates most people isn't physical stature or intellect, but mental toughness."

She unzipped her wetsuit and played with her flippers, putting them on her feet and flipping them off.

"With those flippers on you look like a beautiful mermaid."

"The first time you go through a decompression at this depth, it makes you a bit goofy."

I stepped toward her.

"Don't..." She turned away so I could only see her from the side.

I saw an elfish grin appear on her face. I had made love in a lot of daring places before - the backseat of a Mustang, on a Caribbean beach at sunset, and in a cabin on an airplane a mile high - and it never deterred me. I placed a towel over the inside porthole. Then I pressed my lips against hers, and she melted into my arms.

• • •

The next day I took the sub back to Boston and made my way to our makeshift office. When I entered, Tabitha was sitting at the computer talking to someone through a headset. She hung up and said, "I got news on our embezzlement case."

"Go ahead."

"Ms. McKenzie admitted she took the money to buy a car for her granddaughter. The judge gave her a two-year sentence, but suspended it to time served."

"He must have felt sorry for her," I replied. "At least she doesn't work for that company anymore."

Tabitha seemed pensive for a moment.

I knew she had information on our current case so I asked, "What else?"

She looked up and spoke in a solemn tone, "They found Dr. Lassiter's body off the coast of Greenland. A fisherman thought he had sighted an injured baby whale because it had become bloated with seawater. An autopsy revealed he was immobilized by a toxin right before the accident."

"Do you know what type?"

"An agent that affected his central nervous system."

So the mystery of Dr. Lassiter's death was partly resolved. It was like seeing several cards face up in a game of five-card stud, but there were still a couple cards that were hidden.

"What did you find out about Lassiter at the station?" asked Tabitha.

"Besides the scientific stuff.... He was separated from his wife. They have two children: David and Mary. He lived on Long Island. She lives in upstate New York with the kids. He put in 12 hour days while we work round-the-clock until the case is solved." I winked at her. "I inventoried his possessions and located a day calendar I can use for leads, but there was no journal."

"Rick, a scientist without a journal is like a fish out of water." She smirked. "How was he planning to write his memoirs and get a tax write-off?"

"I don't know. I have a couple other people I need background checks on."

"Sure."

"Cornelius Raymond."

Tabitha tapped the keyboard. "UCLA and graduate school at Cal State. Majors… molecular biology and photosynthesis. PhD thesis on green algae light adaptability."

"Norman Kessler."

"His degree is from the University of Maryland. Both of them. Specialty… microorganisms. Red flag here. He used to work for Hokkaido Corporation. That's a competitor of Consolidated Seed."

"Jody McClinton."

"MIT and Florida State. Biophysics and genetic engineering."

"Jeremy Winston."

"Harvard. General biology, administration, and law." She tilted her head and looked at me with curious eyes. "Rick, what are they doing out there?"

"They're working on the genetic mutation of plants and fish. For example, Trish Conway is trying to breed a subspecies of salmon that can withstand colder temperatures than in its present range."

"There must be a downside to that," she mused. "If you spin off enough subspecies, then you end up with a whole new species. Maybe one that won't fit into the natural environment."

"That's an angle I can work on."

"These guys sound like rich nerds," said Tabitha, "and they're deciding our future."

"Most of them were born into wealthy families, but a few weren't that lucky. They had to work hard to get there. How about Trish? She's from Alabama."

Tabitha leaned her head back. "Do you know who you're talking about? That's Patricia Conway. She led the student effort to divest her college, LSU, from fossil fuels, then she became one of the world's foremost experts on marine biology." She handed a list to me.

"Wow! Look at all these awards she won for her research...Gunther Scientific Achievement Award...special grants from the Department of the Interior...The Brady Prize..."

Tabitha swiveled around in her chair and studied the expression on my face. "You didn't?"

"I did?"

"I guess the smarter they are, the sexier they seem." She giggled, probably picturing Trish as a fat manatee instead of the streamlined harbor seal I knew.

"That's it,' I said. "I'll catch the next sub back to the station. Try to figure out if there is any connection between these folks and Dr. Lassiter. Work up the financials on each one."

• • •

The next morning a line of sunlight fell across the harbor and stopped at the open hatch on the sub's deck. I watched as workmen loaded the supplies - prepackaged meals, scientific gear to conduct tests in the labs, and diving equipment - and wondered why anyone would want to endure an underwater life. I took the sub back to the station and met with Jody. I decided to join him on a dive. We put on scuba gear in lockout chamber # 5, which was on the east side of the undersea station, and waited for the seawater to fill up the space. The process seemed to take forever because Jody was moody and refused to talk, only grunting whenever I asked him a question.

Jody exited the lockout chamber and turned on a strobe light to help guide him. We rode turbo sleds east toward the drop-off of the Continental Shelf. The terrain was more rugged on this side of the station with rocky ridges heaved upward from the bottom and jagged boulders the size of refrigerators. As we cruised down a slope, the visibility became reduced until we could only see 10 yards in front of us. The water was bathed in a royal blue light, hence the name: blue euphotic zone. We set the turbo sleds down by a cairn.

I carried a camera with me and took pictures of everything I saw. There were sponges grouped together in cactus formations, schools of fish darting every which way, and a banded eel about six feet long with alternating light and dark brown rings. I saw fields of faded gray flowers and squids peeking at me from underneath.

Suddenly, a surge of water swept me away. I somersaulted out-of-control and was pushed over a rocky canyon. Below me I saw a drop with no bottom. That bastard had tricked me out onto a ledge.

I swam back toward the plateau. When I got there, Jody was nowhere in sight and no spark was visible from his strobe light. He had left me behind like a dollar coin eaten by a slot machine. I wondered whether he was trying to lose me.

He either went north or south. I turned north and propelled myself with a series of strong flutter kicks. Then I spotted a flicker of yellow from his strobe light. I pulled myself forward with an underwater breaststroke until I could see his body up ahead.

We swam down a gentle slope rimmed with rocks on all sides. An inky-black forest waved in the royal blue atmosphere of this subterranean world. Kelp plants were spaced apart in rows with some of them reaching 20 feet high, the fronds intertwining in a canopy. A few plants remained stunted at less than a foot high. Jody penetrated the forest and I did the same. He weaved in-between the plants and kicked up sand and debris from the bottom. Schools of silver fish meshed together like clouds, barely out of reach. Snails and crabs crawled on the blades of seaweed. A patch of fronds entangled me. I broke their grip with a quick twist of the wrist and settled on the bottom. I noticed mechanical trowel marks on nearby rocks. Jody swam on his back near the top of the canopy, clipping off samples and putting them into a bag. When he was done, I glanced at my watch and determined we had been there about a half hour. We started our turbo sleds and returned to the station just before our air supply ran out.

I didn't get too many answers from him. So when we got back, I walked down the hallway to Dr. Raymond's lab. The scientist was bent over a microscope studying a sample on a slide. Even so I could tell he was a hefty man who worked out once in a while.

He looked up with piercing blue eyes and said bluntly, "I knew you'd come here."

"I hope you don't mean anything by that," I replied. "How far has your research progressed?"

"Right now we're growing different plant samples under the blue light spectrum. We want to reduce the error rate to less than 1%."

"Error rate?"

"There are two types: one, the experiment didn't go as planned or two, a faulty measurement was made."

"What happens when the error rate is less than 1%?"

"We're ready for a field test."

"What do you think about Dr. Lassiter's project?"

His shoulders flinched and his teeth grinded together. He replied, "Dr. Lassiter rushed his experiments into field tests."

"Project Neptune?"

"That experiment should have been shut down based on faulty scientific procedure."

"Did you close it down?"

"No!" He pounded the desk with his fist. "I didn't kill Dr. Lassiter. If I did, I would have strangled him with my bare hands."

I still had one more scientist to interview. I learned a long time ago it was important to know all the players in the poker game before you were dealt a hand. I went back to my quarters and grabbed a printout. When I barged into Dr. Norman Kessler's lab, he was bent over a stack of papers reading something through his thick, dark-rimmed glasses. He muttered without looking up, "Come on in."

I introduced myself and said, "We have information that you first met Dr. Lassiter at a conference in San Diego two years ago."

His eyes lit up. "Indeed, I did."

"And that you used to work for Hokkaido Corporation."

"Consolidated Seed offered me a better benefit package. At my age I have to think about my family."

"Did you discuss your research with him?"

"We did build a rapport at the conference, but I didn't have a chance to collaborate with him."

I unfolded the set of zebra sheets and noted, "According to this security report you tapped into his database twice. Once on July 26 and the second time on August 4."

"I might have accidentally interfaced with another dataset. I was trying to find a back door route into mine. It takes too long to enter the security codes."

"Let me get this straight," I groaned. "You broke into Dr. Lassiter's database two weeks before he was murdered."

"Everyone knows that he's dead. The people down here have been saying that it could have been an accident."

"I don't buy that."

He didn't raise an eyebrow.

I observed that Dr. Kessler was speaking perfect English with rounded vowels and hard consonants. Sometimes when you see someone with a hot hand at the craps table, you have to play a hunch and bet that the roller will hit a number. I decided to do that here. "I've noticed that you have a slight Russian accent underneath your American one."

He paused, then replied, "I was conscripted into the Russian separatist movement in the Ukraine. That is when I emigrated to your country."

We looked squarely at each other.

"I guess you're going to tell me there's a Russian sub out there," he mocked.

"How do you know?"

"When I came back from Martha's Vineyard, the supply sub docked with the U.S.S. Benjamin Franklin. The destroyer is not out here chasing a fishing vessel."

"You don't seem to be surprised?"

"Information is power," he stated. "The United States and Russia intercept emails, phone calls, and internet data all in an effort to accumulate that information. Then both countries use it in nefarious ways."

I went back to Dr. Lassiter's office to look through his desk again and discovered a side drawer that contained about 15 topographical maps. I pulled out each one in turn and unfolded it. The maps showed different underwater regions including depth levels, major ridges or valleys, and mountain ranges. To the west the ocean depth rose as the seabed sloped up to the Atlantic Coast; to the east the plateau plummeted to a depth of two miles. The underwater station was within a half mile of that drop-off point. One map, with faint pencil lines drawn vertically and horizontally to form a grid, showed the various locations of the aquatic gardens that had been planted, but also a dozen other unknown locations. Next to those X markings were different letters and numbers.

Blue lights flashed from a panel attached to the wall. Yellow meant a sub was docking, red was for a fire alert, green meant a diver was in danger, but blue…

Someone burst into the room and yelled, "There's a leak in lockout chamber # 4. We're evacuating to the launch pad."

Water gurgled outside. I folded all the maps together and slid them back into the side drawer. When I stepped into the hallway, cold water splashed up around me from a shallow stream. I hurried toward the main section of the station, but the hatch had been sealed. The wheel that opened the steel door was stuck shut.

People passed by me through an office to another hallway. I followed one of the scientists. Other people ran back toward the leak. A blur streaked past…Dr. Raymond. A dozen of us assembled at the launch pad. One woman tinkered with the instruments in the sub's cockpit.

I pondered the significance of the map with the X markings. The grid must mark distances and travel times, but what about the unknown locations?

The blue lights ceased.

An engineer tramped back into the area with her uniform sopping wet.

A scientist asked, "How bad was it?"

"We lost one of the labs."

I ventured back to Dr. Lassiter's office, sloshing through puddles. The major damage had occurred down the hallway where I heard a cleanup crew working. I grabbed the folded maps and pulled them out of the desk's side drawer. I unfolded a map. Wrong one. I tried again. Still wrong. I systematically went through each one from the first to the last. Nothing. I either imagined the map with the markings or it was gone.

I had a slew of suspects and plenty of motives. It was similar to sitting at a blackjack table with a mix of five card decks before you. There were so many combinations and possibilities that the outcome of the deal was impossible to determine. Thinking that Tabitha could help me sort it out, I decided to take the next sub back to Boston.

Tabitha placed a whole bunch of photos out on the table as though forming the blocks for a wall. A carnival of bright colors burst from them.

"This is not the way it looked underwater."

"I adjusted the light-dark contrast with a photo-enhanced computer program," she said. "This is the way it would actually look underwater if the other shades of light weren't filtered out."

I thought about how the sunlight traveled through the depths of the seawater and the red, orange, green and yellow wavelengths were filtered out until only blue and other dark colors remained. "You're right."

We studied all the photos I had taken in the blue euphotic zone. The cactus-shaped sponges glowed lime-green, the banded eel displayed yellow and crimson rings, the gray flowers had transformed into red anemones with white tentacles, and the squid became pink. Then we looked at the photos taken of the garden of kelp. We could see the way the plot had been carved into the rocky ground like a sculptor etching a stone statue. We noticed a photo where some of the plants had spores of red algae as though affected with a measles virus.

"All's not right with Shangri-La," I said. "What do you think it is?"

"I've been looking at some scientific papers from a conference held in Philadelphia six months ago," said Tabitha. "One scientist in the aquaculture field talked about *Gymnodinium breve*, a type of dinoflagellate, on seaweed. It can lead to accelerated growth of red algae, which releases toxic chemicals into the water."

I realized that when I was on the U.S.S. Benjamin Franklin I did not spot an oil slick in the seawater, but rather the discoloration caused by red algae. Whether or not this came from a plot of kelp, I would have to determine.

Tabitha downloaded the financials on each suspect. Later that morning I met with Brett Holland, an FBI agent just out of Quantico, who was going to make the official arrest. He let me take the lead in the case since I knew who all the suspects were. We traveled back to the undersea station in the evening and decided to lay low until the morning.

I tiptoed to Trish's quarters and tapped on her door. When she let me in, the aroma of perfume lingered everywhere.

She giggled and purred, "I knew you'd come back." She peered at me with eyes that resembled green gems.

I uncorked a bottle of wine I had brought with me, and we drank like two young lovers. I told her how beautiful she was in that moment underneath the sea.

"This is the happiest I've been since I visited Australia with my friend Casey," she said. "We scuba-dived along the Great Reef, camped in the outback, and danced in the waves at a beach near Sydney."

"Mmm...Is that the way you feel now?" I murmured.

"It is, but things change so quickly. When I went back to shore near Sydney, I laid on a towel to get a tan. Then Casey stepped on the spine of a poisonous sea urchin. The lifeguard did all he could, dragging her out of the ocean and giving her CPR, but she died on the beach waiting for the ambulance."

"At the end of my tour in Afghanistan I enjoyed being in-country, walking through the open-air markets, mingling with the local people, and hanging out at the cafes," I said. "Then we went to Helmand Province to meet a tribal chief. As we drove into the town some of us felt it was a trap, but we kept on going. The Taliban opened up with RPGs and small arms from three sides. We called in an airstrike even though we were pinned down. Half of my platoon died. Sometimes when things are going great, stuff happens. You have to pick yourself up afterwards and keep going."

We shared the wine and small talk for about an hour. There is something about a woman clinging to me that makes me sleep soundly afterwards. I knew that when I woke up I would be ready to roll.

• • •

At 7 a.m. Brett and I barged into Jody's quarters unannounced, the door banging against its steel frame. We saw him sitting on the edge of his bunk.

Jody looked up and growled, "What do you guys want?"

"You got a quarter million dollars stashed in a bank account in the Cayman Islands," I stated. "Maybe you hit the state lottery. Hey!"

He sat still and didn't say anything.

"You spent that 10 minutes cleaning rock samples and placing them in the collection bin."

Jody stirred and said, "So we did a little mining. Nickel, chromium, it's all over the place."

"You're under arrest for unauthorized use of company property."

"And for murder," stated Brett.

I give him a harsh look.

Jody hung his head and said, "I didn't kill Dr. Lassiter."

"No?" gasped the FBI agent.

I stepped toward Jody and pulled out a pair of plastic handcuffs. The FBI agent drew his Taser and moved forward.

Jody kicked the Taser out of Brett's hand, threw him against the wall with a thud, and dashed off.

I spun around and sprinted after him, going past Brett, who was slumped on the floor and dazed. The FBI stiff didn't understand the stakes everyone was playing for. When you play a game of poker and pile all the chips in the table's center, anything can happen.

I chased Jody down the hallway.

The sub's launch pad was only 30 yards away. If he could close its hatch before I caught him, he would have a chance of getting free. I dove at him. My hands caught his feet and tripped him.

Jody fell, but crawled toward the open hatch. He dropped down head first.

I lunged forward and pinned his waist against the opening.

He struggled like a slippery fish and squirmed loose, banging on the floor below.

I dropped down feet first and sunk to my knees. When I stood up, he started throwing punches. I caught them in my open hands before they struck my body or face, the smacks echoing off the sub's walls. My training in Tai Chi helped me keep my composure.

Jody swerved, throwing one punch after another.

I slipped a punch and grabbed his arm. Using his own forward momentum, I tossed him against the steel hull.

He crashed into the wall, but bounced up and kept flailing away.

I tossed him one way then another.

After the third toss against the steel hull, he collapsed to the ground in pain.

I stepped over him and slipped on the plastic handcuffs.

The FBI agent took him back to Boston in the sub, but I stayed on at the station. Even though Jody probably killed Dr. Lassiter, I had to cover all the angles, like a player drawing cards for a poker hand. I ran into Trish after breakfast and told her I wanted to inspect the plot of kelp in the blue euphotic zone again.

"You've already seen it," she said. "And you have a suspect. Why not leave well enough alone?"

"The plot of kelp they were cultivating in the blue euphotic zone was infected with red algae. I need to take another look to see if that would give someone else a motive to kill Dr. Lassiter."

"Are you finding excuses to hang around with me?" she teased.

"I wish I were."

We began strolling toward lockout chamber # 5. She stopped and said, "Defective seaweed causes red tide blooms that contaminate shellfish and lead to massive fish kills. Groups like the Free Oceans Network are trying to stop that. You would be doing everyone a favor if you let Project Neptune die."

"I'm not ready to fold," I countered. "I play the game until the bank is broke or I'm broke."

We suited up in the lockout chamber. As seawater filled the chamber, I checked my tank and gave Trish the thumbs up. We swam outside and got turbo sleds from the storage shed. We scooted east toward the Continental Shelf over barren terrain with only sparse concentrations of sponges and anemones. We came to the black forest in the blue euphotic zone and slowed down. I dropped my spear gun by the turbo sled and explored a section of the garden that had those markings along the ground. I noticed a broken piece of Plexiglas embedded in the sand. I pulled it out and traced the outline of a foundation in the rock and sand. A fish pen had been in the blue euphotic zone. Trish had known what was going on all along. The first red algae bloom had killed the designer fish she was studying. I spun around.

She raised her spear gun, her eyes set in an icy glare.

I lifted the Plexiglas shield just in time. The spear sizzled through the water and glanced off, grazing my shoulder.

Trish loaded another spear into the gun.

I was too far away to rush her so I spun around and swam. I brushed against one plant and then another. I swam among the fronds and circled around the trunks. Another spear sizzled through the water, going underneath my belly. I turned off the strobe light so Trish couldn't see me. I made my way through the black forest by flutter kicking with my feet and groping with my hands to keep from being entangled. I swam past the boundary and found myself over a canyon. Water pushed me up into a somersault. I swam back to the plants and traced the perimeter of the plot.

When I returned to our entry point, I turned on the strobe light. Trish was gone. She had given me a warning in her own way, and I had ignored it. The southern belle was a femme fatale.

I crawled along the bottom to the turbo sled and saw a bunch of wires sticking out. Trish had disabled the controls. I began swimming back to the undersea station. I had made it about half way when I realized I only had a couple gulps of air left.

I knew I couldn't make it back to the undersea station before the tank ran out so I decided to float up to the surface. Stretching out my arms, I closed my eyes and flapped my flippers to gently rise. I remembered a mantra taught to me by a yoga and hummed to myself, the last bubbles of tri-mix rising above me. When I broke the surface, the sun's glare almost blinded me. Tears came out of my eyes and fogged up my visor as I adjusted to the bright sunshine bearing down on me and reflecting off the ocean. I gazed in every direction and saw seawater all around me. Nothing else was in sight. I still had two cards left to play.

I'd been in a difficult situation like this before. After I took out an Al-Qaeda cell in Libya, I trudged through the Sahara Desert for seven days with only a goat skin filled with wine. That job was for a major oil company. Who said that all multi-nationals were bad? There were swells on the ocean a few feet deep. Sometimes I rose to the top of one and other times sunk to the bottom. I treaded water with my feet and held my waterproof watch high in the air. I dialed back to base.

"This is Barrett," I said. "Send out an S.O.S." I gave Tabitha my latitude and longitude.

"The SOS has been sent out," she said. "Rick, are you on the destroyer?"

"Negative."

"What type of boat are you on? The reception is terrible."

"I'm treading water above the undersea station."

"No!" she gasped. "How did that happen?"

"Trish Conway. Put out an APB on her. She just tried to kill me."

A moment later Tabitha replied, "Done. Do you want me to stay on the line until help comes? It could take a while until they find you."

"Negative. I'll make do." I clicked off the phone. The $8,000 I paid for it had been justified. I got my bearings again. I had drifted off my original latitude and longitude already. I swam a freestyle stroke with my head held above the seawater. When I got a bit west of my original position, I sucked in a deep breath and thrust my arms out as though on a cross. I floated on my back while meditating. I had to take turns conserving my energy. I could probably last out here for a day or two at most. My hope was that the U.S.S. Benjamin Franklin or a coast guard cutter could find me within a half day.

Whenever I floated on my back, I lapsed into a daydream. I dreamed about picking peaches in an orchard when I was young and biting into the tart fruit with the juice spilling down my chin. I saw myself on my first Harley Davidson, winding through the Pocono Mountains of Pennsylvania, with the breeze ruffling my hair. Everything was going easy when I saw it.

A shark's dorsal fin was only 20 yards away. Several more sliced across the surface not far behind. My little flutter kick and wiggling of arms had attracted them. It was time to stand my ground. I could either play possum or fight. I decided to play possum first. I kept my legs together and bobbed in the seawater, trying to look like a piece of driftwood. The blue sharks began to circle. I could see their teeth gleaming just under the surface. One came near and swam away. Another approached and veered in the opposite direction. I could take my flare gun out of its dry pack and shoot the next one at point blank range to scare them off, but to what advantage? My last card would be played. I was just a speck on the ocean and would need the flare to alert a ship or search helicopter. What good was beating off the shark pack only to be lost at sea?

Suddenly, I saw a speck of gray on the horizon coming closer and closer. When I made the outline of a ship, I took out my flare gun and held it above the seawater. I squeezed the trigger and the flare zoomed ten stories high and exploded like a rainbow maker on the 4th of July. The ship kept coming closer and closer and so did the sharks. One nipped at my wetsuit. I beat the seawater with my fist. Another darted in from the opposite side. I thrust my mask in its face, making it veer away. The circle was drawing tighter and tighter and their mouths were gaping open, ready to strike.

There was an explosion underwater with a mound of seawater and the sound coming up to the surface about a quarter mile behind the vessel. A bigger boom followed. Either the destroyer had dropped a depth charge that hit the sub or something awful had happened at the undersea station. Ripples fanned out from the epicenter that caused me to bob up and down harder in the seawater. The sharks scattered and disappeared under the surface. I thought about all the things that could happen on the seabed - fish farming, aquatic gardening, mining for minerals, and the shaping of man-made islands - and how it could one day lead to wars all around the world.

The ship was getting closer. I could see several sailors dressed in their white uniforms leaning over the bow and pointing at me. It looked a bit different than when I last saw it. The gun turret and missile batteries were the same, but now two helicopters were perched on the landing site in the stern. The ship veered in an arc. When the vessel turned broadside, I realized I had made a mistake. It was not flying the Stars and Stripes, but a tricolor flag with broad horizontal stripes and had strange markings on its side. As I treaded seawater in the ocean, I waited for the Russian warship to drop a lifeboat, if it would.

Ceremonious Cicadas

During rehearsal the garden beside our church was a bastion of tranquility with the fragrance of flowers in full bloom and the chirping of birds coming from a nearby grove of oak trees. A week later that had changed. On the day of our wedding a sizzling sound came from all around as thousands of cicadas, who had emerged from the ground as part of their 17-year life cycle, clung to the leaves of trees and bushes. Cicadas flew from one tree to another in search of mates, sometimes buzzing through the air on low trajectories that took them close to the ground. Wedding guests ducked and turned sideways to elude the stubby black insects. I heard my aunt say, "Those tulips look lovely this time of year." Then I saw her step out of the way of an incoming cicada. But we had to stay put because this was the place where we would conclude our wedding ceremony with a releasing of the doves.

I was holding the hand on my newlywed wife. She whispered, "It's just a small hiccup in our plans." From the corner on my eye I could see bugs swooping through the air. I even had to brush one off my beloved's white gown.

The minister walked down the brick lane carrying a wicker basket. Inside a pair of white doves were cooing. The minister stopped by the fountain in the middle of the garden and talked about the importance of carrying out our wedding vows. He lifted the lid and announced, "With the release of these doves, we signify that your marriage will be one of peace and harmony."

The doves did not fly off. Instead they hunkered down inside the basket as cicadas whirled by. Again the minister repeated the words in a solemn voice. This time he tapped the basket. Nothing happened. The doves wouldn't budge.

All the wedding guests leaned this way and that. They were not trying to get a better view, but dodged the cicadas swarming everywhere. My aunt shrieked when she saw a red-eyed bug crawling up her dress. A bridesmaid buckled at the knees and almost fainted. My brother rolled up the wedding program and swung it through the air like a baseball bat, belting bugs over the garden like Barry Bonds slugging homers.

"Let's go." The minister flipped the basket upside down and shook it.

The doves hung onto the willow strips with their heads swiveling every which way, wary of the cicada invasion. Their cooing had been replaced with deep-throated grunts.

"I said, get out you dumb doves!" screamed the minister. "Show this couple what peace and harmony is all about!" He whacked the bottom of the basket several times with each swat louder than the last.

The doves shrieked in terror and took flight, darting sideways to avoid the dive-bombing cicadas. One of them smacked into the side of the church, losing a bunch of feathers as though a pillow had been punctured.

It has been two weeks now and my hand still trembles when I recall that part of the ceremony. But I don't plan to get the marriage annulled because we sealed the deal with a kiss. And every time one of us starts to remember, the other is there with a squeeze and a smooch to make us forget.

Bear of the Bog

TIM TOM SPOTTED SCRATCH marks on a red oak and a paw print in the mud. "There's a bear around here," he warned. "Let's stick together." The hikers shortened the distance between them until they were lined up as close as bowling pins. They hiked down the ridge of Saddleback Mountain and followed him into a valley with damp underbrush and a lingering scent of wildflowers.

The lead dog, Oscar, an Austrian shepherd five feet long with a husky build and brownish-black fur, caught the animal's scent and pointed with its snout. Another dog, Scout, trotted toward the end of the line. Scout was a white lab with a gentle disposition, always licking or rubbing up against people on the trail, but this time he didn't do a U-turn to get upfront again.

"Black bear," gasped Ryan. He stopped and pointed to the left, "At ten o'clock."

"Stop here," ordered Tim Tom. "He's not that far away."

The hikers dropped their backpacks and drank from water bottles, sweat dotting their clothes and beading up on their brows. They watched a black bear dig up plants in the gully and chew on roots with its butt wagging over the trail. The odor of salami filled the air.

"Mary, what are you doing!?" screamed Tim Tom. "There's a bear down there!"

"I'm sorry." She was sitting on a log with a sandwich on her lap, and a couple bites taken out. "I wasn't hungry when we stopped for lunch. I've been listening to my stomach rumble for the last mile and thought I could eat while we waited."

Tim Tom snarled through clenched teeth, "That odor is going to draw him over here."

"I thought we were downwind," she said apologetically, rewrapping it.

The bear meandered from one side of the trail to the other. At one point it stood up on its hind legs and gazed in their direction.

"Don't say nothing," whispered Tim Tom. "Be quiet."

They stood as rigid as the red oaks and tulip poplars surrounding them and held their breaths for what seemed like forever. The bear dropped down on all fours and ambled over the ridge. The hikers scooted past where it had been. When they got over the next hill, Tim Tom sighed with relief. "Never do that again, Mary. Promise me."

"I won't."

"If that bear had caught our scent, it would have meant trouble. We're lucky he didn't notice us."

But it was too late. The Bear of the Bog was smitten with Mary. He liked her black T-shirt and the way her curly brown hair laid on her shoulders and how her cheeks were flush with the color of ripe apples. And he couldn't get the smell of salami out of his nostrils. It was more powerful than the scent of other bears. But he couldn't understand why this female walked on her hind legs like a human. Was she imitating the upright stature of the albino bear leading her? The Bear of the Bog was prepared to follow her wherever she went and to fight the albino for the privilege of mating.

They heard twigs snapping nearby. Iggy and Blossom wandered out of the woods. Iggy had scraggly black hair that hung to his shoulders and a beard as tangled as a bird's nest. Every time he took a step he jangled because of bells fastened to his shirt and one dangling from his left ear. Blossom intertwined a wreath of mountain laurel in her fiery-red hair like a tiara. Their two dogs, Max, a cross between a Rottweiler and a Ridgeback, and Samantha, a little bull terrier saved from a Humane Society shelter, padded about.

"Where's this Dan coming from?" asked Ryan. "I can smell something on him a mile away."

"Hold your fire," said Tim Tom. "I'll see."

The couple walked closer.

"Where were you guys?" screamed Tim Tom. "We just saw a bear.'

"A bear?" they asked.

"Yes, a black bear. Back there about a half klick."

Blossom held up a wicker basket full of jagged green plants. "We were picking some weed. It grows wild out here."

"Smoke this," said Iggy, "and you'll see colors you've never dreamed of."

"I'm not into that junk," said Tim Tom. "You have changed since we served in the Gulf. What happened?"

"Nothing happened, Tom-Tom. I've always been laid back, but you can't show that side of yourself when you're going through Basic or have al-Qaeda shooting at you."

"You know my name," roared Tim Tom.

"Hey, man, it just slipped out. You know, like you're a drum, Tom-Tom, or something."

Tim Tom stepped forward, his 6'5" frame towering over Iggy. He had a hard body pumped up with weight lifting and could bench press 295 pounds and squat 600. In Iraq he was the blonde-haired marine always called upon to bust down a door or pry open a locked box. And his name, Timothy Thomas, had been shortened to a compact Tim Tom like a short punch to the ribs. He balled his hand into a fist. "Do I have to clobber you?"

"Come on, Tim Tom, relax," said Mary as she held him back. "We're having a reunion."

"You keep messing with me," he snarled, "and you'll be lying on the ground looking up."

Iggy was playing with the plants in the basket. "Hey, Blossom, what do you think? We can smoke some weed tonight and do a little star gazing."

"I'm down," she said. "Somebody's got to chill around here."

"Let's keep moving," demanded Tim Tom, "before that bear comes back."

"Oh, honey," chuckled Mary. "He went away a long time ago."

Ryan checked his watch. "It's only been 20 minutes."

"Hey, man," said Iggy, "you wouldn't worry about bears if you sang songs or wore bells. That's what keeps them away."

"I ain't wearing no jingle bells," sneered Tim Tom.

"He's a bit old-fashioned," said Mary. "Maybe you guys could lead us in a sing-along."

"Sure...." They goofily grinned and bobbed their heads.

For the rest of the afternoon Iggy and Blossom lead them through old hippie ballads. One of their favorites went like this:

> *When the moon is in the Seventh House*
> *And Jupiter aligns with Mars*
> *Then peace will guide the planets*
> *And love will steer the stars*
>
> *This is the dawning of the Age of Aquarius*
> *The Age of Aquarius*
> *Aquarius...Aquarius!*

And all their voices, whether nasal or gravelly or off-pitch or scratchy, were blended together in the spirit of communion.

The Bear of the Bog had never heard something so dreadful. He was used to hearing birds chirping and whistling, the hum of bees, and even the creaking of crickets which did not sound as bad. But the noise that came forth from their mouths made them easy to follow because he could hear it a quarter mile away.

They were tramping through a bog with patches of skunk cabbage and swarms of gnats swirling all around. Tim Tom looked down at his white T-shirt and saw a dozen mosquitoes trying to puncture through. "Hey, Ryan, toss me that bug dope."

Ryan flipped him the can. "Now we know what those old timers in 'Nam had to go through. It can't get any worse than this."

Just then the bear growled and cut across the path behind them. He was making his move, trying to separate the female bear with the salami smell from her pack. He had waited long enough, and the hormones in his loins were throbbing and his stomach aching.

"Let's get going," yelled Ryan as he grabbed his gear and marched double-time.

The dogs barked and howled.

"Hey, man, what's going on?" asked Iggy. "Did you see that cloud's shadow drifting across the trail?"

"That wasn't a shadow," said Tim Tom. "It was the bear. Get moving!"

Mary called from the rear, "Tim Tom, help me! Help!"

"Oscar! Max! Let's go!" Tim Tom and the dogs raced back. Instead of following the trail as it wound its way up and down slopes and in and around trees, they splashed through black pools of water and bushes up to the top of Tim Tom's thighs. When they reached Mary, she was still screaming.

The bear was only ten yards away, baring its fangs and drooling at the mouth.

"Get out!" yelled Tim Tom as he and the dogs charged, "Get out!"

The Bear of the Bog galloped through bushes, hoping his new girlfriend would follow, but instead the female of his fantasies merely hunkered down. The bear looped around the albino bear and headed back toward its sweetheart.

Tim Tom shot the bug spray, hoping to blind the animal, but it lingered in the air like a misty fog and settled on nearby bushes.

Mary regained her composure. Now fright bellowed inside of her, *Run!* She took off down the trail as fast as she could go.

The dogs dashed in loops and barked. Tim Tom tried to track the bear's footprints, tramping through thorn bushes. When he caught up to Mary, she was a quarter mile down the trail with the rest of their group. His jeans were splattered with mud and studded with thorns. "We scared him off for a while."

But the Bear of the Bog wasn't scared at all. His first thought was, *Where's my lady love?* as he was drawn by that salami smell. But the more he circled this way or that, the less certain he was of where he was going. He stopped in a gully and wondered *Which way have I come?* He had made so many turns, he had ended up confusing himself.

"We got to get ahead of that bear," said Tim Tom.

The next mountain in Shenandoah National Park had a 1,600 feet gain in elevation over three miles. The first slope was seven tenths of a mile with a flat part in the middle, but the second slope climbed for more than two miles and included a switchback that just keep going up and up. Tim Tom marched onward without once looking back, but the other hikers pulled out of line to catch their breath two, three, sometimes four different times. They hunched over and sucked in air until their ribs stopped throbbing in pain and their legs stopped feeling like dead weights. Even Ryan, who had a jogger's wiry frame, stopped once to catch his breath. But Tim Tom hiked up the hill so fast he waited 15 minutes for everybody else to show up. By the time the last straggler arrived at the top, three dogs had fallen asleep: Oscar's feet stuck up in the air, Max lay on the ground flatter than a log, and Scout was snoozing in Mary's lap. Ryan asked, "Are they sleeping or dead?"

"Those lazy good-for-nothings are sleeping," complained Tim Tom. "That's what we get for pampering them."

"Samantha's ready to go," said Blossom.

And it was true. Samantha was darting in and out of bushes. The bull terrier still had too much pup in her to realize she should be tired.

They picked up their backpacks and humped along a ridge, and off, in the distance, saw the Blue Ridge's spine sticking up like the scales of a prehistoric dinosaur. The sun settled in a maroon pool on the horizon, but its last light reflected off the sky above. When blackness crept upon them, Tim Tom walked into a clearing and yelled, "Let's pitch camp." The men got out their head lamps and set up tents with their lights shining as brightly as coal miners. The women gathered twigs and fallen branches, which seemed to be laying everywhere, and built a fire which hissed and crackled.

The campfire was five feet in diameter and surrounded by a ring of stones. The flame shot up a foot and a half high and was golden-orange, leaping and dancing with delight. The logs blackened as the flame curled round them and a bed of white ash formed. Several feet out the campers sat on makeshift chairs made from flat rocks or logs. They drank elderberry wine Blossom had made and listened to Mary's iPhone. The girls sang karaoke to the tunes, their favorites being from the Eagles or Billy Joel. The guys told stories about their tours in the Gulf. Tim Tom said, "There's one thing I learned in Bagdad from seeing all the dead bodies and blood splattered after a roadside bomb went off and the families bawling over their loved ones. You only live once…so enjoy your life while you can."

"I'll second that," agreed Ryan. "Enjoy every day of your life."

They all clinked their plastic cups.

Blossom and Iggy strayed from the fire to smoke some weed.

"Look up there," said Blossom. "Aren't those stars beautiful?"

"As beautiful as the ones on our flag," said Iggy.

The couple hugged and locked their lips in a kiss.

Back at the fire Mary was peering at a nearby grove of trees, "What's that?"

"What's what?" said Ryan.

"That shadow over there. An animal or something."

"Where?" asked Tim Tom.

"Over there."

A growling sound came from the trees.

"It's the bear. He's trying to get into our food bag." Tim Tom picked up a skillet and a pot and banged them together and shouted, "Hey, get away from there."

The bear bared its fangs and growled.

Tim Tom backed up toward the fire whose flame promised protection.

The other campers came over with their dogs pacing back and forth, barking at a frenzied pitch. "What's going on?"

"That bear is stealing our food. It's time to send the cavalry in," ordered Tim Tom. "Let's round them up."

"You can't do that to him," said Blossom.

"The hell we can't."

Their cries went out: "Oscar!" "Max!" "Scout!" "Samantha!" Each owner held onto the collar of their dog and made them stand at attention. The dogs were frothing at the mouth in anticipation of defending their master or mistress and doing battle. Tim Tom issued the command, "Oscar, and you other dogs, …go get him!"

They scampered toward their prey barking and howling.

The bear retreated downhill.

"We got him now!" yelled Ryan.

"Look at him go," laughed Iggy.

The bear went maybe 40 yards and turned around when he came to familiar territory by the woods. The animals disappeared from view beyond the fire's glow. The campers could only hear the confrontation as a series of growls, barks, howls, and yelps.

Oscar was the biggest dog, but not the most courageous so he faded behind the pack. So did Scout because all he could handle were dead ducks and geese. Even the flapping of a wing from a wounded bird was enough to make him shy away. That meant Max took the lead with little Samantha behind him. Max lowered his snout so he could get underneath the bear and bite its neck, but the bear flipped him over with its paw. He somersaulted through the air and landed a foot away with a thud.

The creature spun around and chomped on his rear end.

Max yelped and raced uphill. So did Oscar and Scout when they saw how huge the bear was. Only little Samantha stayed behind. She had too much pup in her to realize she was supposed to be scared. And weren't all other animals bigger than her anyway? She dipped to the right and took a snip and then to the left. Fur went flying everywhere.

The Bear of the Bog had only seen an animal like this once before: a badger protecting its lair from a pack of wolves. Even though the badger was outnumbered seven to one, it fought with such grit it held the pack at bay. This little animal came alive with the same spirit. The bear was about to give up and head back home when he got an unexpected source of help.

Max returned to camp whimpering in fright, then Scout slumbered in not saying anything, and finally Oscar showed up and sallied around and barked as though he had put up a fight.

"Where's Sam? Do you see Sam?" screeched Blossom. "The bear's going to maul her." She screamed, "Samantha, come back here! Come back!"

The little dog stopped fending off the bear and lifted her head to make sure her mistress was calling. Then she rushed back to camp.

When Blossom saw her dog, she ran over and hugged her and wept, "Sam, did they leave you all alone. Poor darling. You could have been hurt."

The bear ambled up the hill to see what was going on. The campers were huddled near the fire with the dogs trotting in circles around them.

"He's coming back," cautioned Ryan. "What are we going to do?"

"Get out of my way," said Tim Tom as he trudged past the others. He put on his gloves, reached into the campfire's flames, and picked up two burning logs. When he waved them about, it looked as though he was twirling burning batons with red ambers flying off like 4th of July sparklers.

The Bear of the Bog saw the albino bear standing on his hind legs waving the sticks. He was not afraid, but was tired from trying to outflank that pesky dog. And he was so sleepy he was leaning to one side. So he plodded down the hill, curled up in a hollow tree trunk, and decided to sleep until daybreak.

"Thanks for the demonstration, man," said Iggy. "That was super-cool. Just like a laser show for a rock band."

"I'm not trying to entertain you," said Tim Tom. "Don't you know how dangerous bears are?'

"Hey, man, all you got to do is wear bells to scare him off." Iggy got up and pranced around the campfire with the bells jiggling all over him.

"Screw your bells."

The next morning a skimpy layer of cirrus clouds blotted out the sun and any patch of blue. On the plateau the wind whistled an eerie tune and a foul odor came from the pines surrounding the campsite which had withered from disease or died. The dead ones were stripped of their bark and dotted with woodpecker holes. Branches had been snapped off from storms and lay about everywhere. It was a graveyard of trees where crows gathered and cawed and ruffled their wings.

Tim Tom was brewing a pot of coffee on the bonfire's coals when he heard someone hollering from the bottom of the hill. Iggy and Blossom dropped their baskets and hustled into camp with their bells jingling and their bodies trembling with fear.

"He's coming, man," gasped Iggy, "He's coming."

"Who's coming?"

Blossom squeezed out the words between her panting, "The bear. He's huge."

Grrrrr…came a sound from downhill. The bear was within 50 yards and closing. It picked up a branch in its teeth and thrashed it against a rock, smashing one end apart.

They grabbed their gear and galloped the other way. Blossom called out, "Run, Tim Tom, run."

The other campers and dogs scampered for cover behind a mound of rocks, but Tim Tom snarled, "I've served two tours in the Gulf. I'm not running from nothing. He's trying to scare us." He crouched down and sprinted forward like a football player heading toward a tackling sled and rammed into the trunk of a dead tree at least a hundred feet tall. Dirt flew into the air as the roots popped out. The tree tilted and came crashing down with a whoosh…boom. The ground shook like Jell-O and a cloud of dust mushroomed.

The bear dropped its branch and stood up on its hind legs. Then it turned around and rambled downhill.

The campers cheered and the dogs howled.

The bear hightailed it back to the bog where he was born. The odor of salami was finally blown out of his nostrils. He knew that one day he would mate and raise a family. What he didn't know was that he would always be haunted by the memory of the great albino bear.

A Hero for Herons

"THERE IT IS!" shouted Ingrid, whose fingers tapped on the dashboard. His wife had seen the burgundy awning of the Madeleine Truffaut Beauty Salon. "Park over there."

Hamilton rocked the car back and forth until it fit into a spot nearby. His wife leaped out of the seat and dashed inside while he fumbled in his pocket for quarters to feed the meter. Then he slipped into the salon himself. The proprietor, a small lady with short black hair styled into a sassy perm, was wearing a ruffled dress and spoke in a French accent. The stylists who cut and fashioned the hairdos were mostly women except for one man with feminine manners and a high-pitched voice. Hamilton sat in a chair and picked up a magazine, content to wait for the next hour. His wife was in the back getting her hair shampooed. He saw women having tonics rubbed into their hair, curlers set to produce wavy styles, and even wads of tinfoil, like gum wrappers, pasted to one woman's strands. Soon the odor of perfume overwhelmed his nose and the women gossiping about relationships grated on his ears. He stood up and told the receptionist, "Tell Ingrid I'll be back in an hour."

Hamilton left the salon and shuffled down the street. At the corner several cars were backed up at a street light. Shoppers gazed at displays that filled pictures windows or hustled out of stores carrying bags. He crossed the street and saw pedestrians walking behind the shops. He cut down an alley and discovered a walkway along a cement canal with water flowing in a chute toward the end of town. As he walked along, he noticed little gardens with cardinal-red irises and other brightly colored flowers springing up alongside the canal. When he got to a ten-foot high footbridge arching over the canal, he climbed to the top. The water was flowing from the west to the east right through the heart of Frederick toward the Monocacy River. Hamilton didn't know there was a connection between the rain and streams gurgling down mountainsides and the river rushing through this canal. Water was just something that came from a pipe or he bought in bottles at the grocery store. Once he had a chance to take a sailing trip on the Potomac River, but when he saw the boat bobbing in choppy water, he became too scared to board. He came down from that dizzying height and continued his journey upstream.

Two people hustled toward him. The first was a man in a white uniform more appropriate for a safari on a grassy plain in Kenya. The man had a canteen fastened to his belt and a pair of binoculars hanging from his neck. He cried out, "Mister, can you tell us which way the goldfinch went?"

"What's a goldfinch?" asked Hamilton.

A petite woman dressed in blue tennis shorts and a blue visor came up to him and said, "It looks like a yellow parakeet." She was weighted down with similar gear, but held a birding guide in her hand.

"I didn't notice," he said.

"How can you not notice?" howled the safari man. Then he hollered, "I'll go up the canal and you go down. If you see him, buzz my cell phone."

"We'll find him," said the woman, who dashed across the footbridge.

Hamilton had to cross a street to follow the canal. He heard children squealing and saw them romping a short distance away. When he saw Baker Park with its wide expanse of green grass spread before him, he was amazed. The only green he had seen growing up in the suburbs of Washington, D.C. were manicured lawns surrounded by hedges. And the only wildlife he had ever seen were gray squirrels scurrying about and an occasional robin or sparrow chirping from a tree branch or building ledge. Even the place he worked at in Bethesda was surrounded by other high-rise office buildings. He walked close to the trickling water of the canal, dodging a lady pushing a pram and a jogger in shorts and a T-shirt. He looked into the canal at the smooth flow of water. Then he saw a bird three feet tall with a yellow beak.

The creature did not notice him, but stared at a spout of water as though mesmerized by the flow.

Hamilton knew the bird was too big to be a goldfinch and not the right color. He was about to sit down at a nearby bench when he remembered dropping off his wife at the salon. Oh my God, he thought, her appointment is over. He retraced his steps, occasional skipping along the sidewalk to get back quicker. When he got back to the salon, his wife was standing under the shadow cast by its awning, shielding her face and arms which were of a light complexion and easily sunburned.

"I'm sorry," he said. "I lost track of time. You wouldn't believe what I saw."

"Your brother is back from Afghanistan?"

"No, he's still there," said Hamilton. "I mean in the park. I saw this really big bird...like a penguin."

"You saw a penguin in the park?"

"No. Yes. I mean..."

"Did you stop in at the James Joyce Pub for a mug of Irish stout?"

"I haven't been drinking," he said, looking at the shamrock-green awning of the nearby pub. He shook his head as though confused and said, "I saw a penguin in the park."

"Do you see any snow or ice around here?" asked his wife. "Do you think we're living in Antarctica?"

"No, nothing like that."

"Buster, I can't take you anywhere."

On the ride home Ingrid wouldn't say a word. He only knew she was sitting next to him by the fragrant smell coming from her hair. After they entered their living room, she peered at him as though he was a deranged psycho in a movie and said, "You need to see my brother."

"There's nothing wrong with me," he replied.

"You imagine you saw a penguin in the park?"

He sighed. "Okay, I'll go see him."

The following Wednesday, Hamilton marched into his boss's office with his hand placed on his back and tilting forward like an old man. He groaned, "A pain is shooting up my spine. I set up a doctor's appointment for this afternoon."

"I hope it gets better," said his boss. "I threw out my back several years ago on a skiing trip in Breckenridge. I had to take painkillers for a month."

"Thanks for understanding."

Hamilton left his office after lunch and took the elevator down to the lobby. Even though the skyscraper he was going to was only two streets away, he walked in the opposite direction for several blocks, over one street, past the rear of his office building, and to the place where his brother-in-law worked. He didn't want anybody to know he was coping with a psychological ailment. Upon finding Bradley Street, he scooted into the skyscraper when nobody was looking and rode the elevator up to the eighth floor. He strolled down the hallway until he saw a placard that read: *Erik Olsson* Life Coach. He knocked on the door and entered the office.

His brother-in-law welcomed him inside and sat behind a desk with a smoky-glass top. Even though Erik was only in his 30s he had a long, withered face and a scraggly, ash-blonde beard. "I normally charge $200 an hour," he said, "but since you are *family* I will give you a 25% discount. Please excuse me while I finish my call." Erik picked up the phone and began talking to someone as though in mid-conversation.

Hamilton thought about leaving, then saw a wall covered with degrees from various programs all over the world including a yoga instructor certificate from an ashram in New Delhi, a scuba diver license from Brisbane, Australia, an Enlightened Spirit certificate awarded for ascending the trail to Machu Picchu in Peru, and a sweat lodge operator license earned on a Lakota reservation in South Dakota. So he turned around and plopped in a chair across from the desk.

Erik hung up the phone, looked at him, and asked, "Why are you here?"

Hamilton didn't know how to tell him about his problem. He got up and paced the room. Then he said, "I've been seeing things that aren't there. I took Ingrid to the hairdresser last Saturday and went for a walk in Baker Park. I thought I saw a giant bird in a ditch. It was as big as a penguin, but I don't know if it could waddle or not."

"Hmmm," murmured Erik.

"You don't think that's unusual?"

"Yes and no," he replied. "Hamilton, come over here."

Hamilton walked over to the window where Erik was gazing out.

"I've seen tigers in a game preserve in India, kangaroos in the outback of Australia, and free-roaming bison on the great plains in this country. But what you are describing is beyond farfetched." Erik pointed at something through the window and asked, "What do you see down there?"

Hamilton spotted a little patch of green in-between the tall office buildings and said, "It's a park."

"Do you think there's a big bird in that park?"

"No."

Erik turned to him and explained, "Delusion is a coping mechanism humans use to overcome disappointment. If we don't get a promotion at work, we think the boss gave it to someone else because of nepotism. If we don't take the prettiest girl to the prom, we think that they are not smart enough to keep up with a man like us. But when it takes over your life and you see things that are not there, it becomes a problem. I counselled one woman who had to contact a spiritual medium every day before she could make a move. And I coached a man that bought $500 worth of lottery tickets every week because he thought he could become a billionaire. The first thing you need to do is to distinguish reality from fantasy when the time comes. Here are the six simple steps to overcome a delusional episode." He handed him a card.

Hamilton placed it in his shirt pocket and said, "I want to thank you for helping me to sort this thing out."

"No problem at all," said Erik. "I'll schedule another appointment for you next month so we can drill down into your core and discover what makes you tick."

"Oh, yeah," replied Hamilton hesitantly, wondering what his wife had gotten him into.

Ingrid's hair grew out until she got upturned ends that made it look curly when she woke up in the morning. She had to comb it straight before going to work. Then the strands became too wavy to manage even with a bristle brush or styling gel. After three weeks she couldn't maintain the hairdo she wanted. On a Saturday Hamilton drove her back to Madeleine Truffaut's Beauty Salon feeling a sense of composure on the way because he believed his wildlife sighting was a mirage triggered by stress. So he decided not to stay too long in the salon least he be agitated by the overwhelming perfumes and the women's banter about relationships. Plus, he had the card given to him by his brother-in-law to help him cope with a delusional episode.

After he dropped off his wife, he trotted along the canal dripping sweat because summer had arrived. He could hear children playing in the park and the reassuring sound of cars motoring on nearby streets. Civilization was only a stone's throw away. He listened to the water percolating through the canal as he ambled upstream. He felt good inside and thought about a pop song's melody he had heard on the radio driving over. Then he saw it. No! It couldn't be. The bird, which was three feet high with bluish-gray feathers and a yellow beak, stood in the bottom of the canal looking at the water pouring down a miniature waterfall.

Hamilton's hand trembled as he pulled out the card from his shirt pocket. He held on with both hands to keep it still and began implementing the six steps to overcome this delusional episode. He sucked in a deep breath and then another one. He started at the number 20 and counted backwards until he reached 0. He repeated, "My name is Hamilton and I am 26 years old." He took another deep breath. He pinched a wad of skin near his wrist until he felt a little pain. He centered his thoughts around one meme - *I am in control.* Then he turned his head and looked into the canal again.

The bird was still there. It hadn't moved and was a big as he first imagined. He shook his head and screamed, "Ah!"

Hamilton scanned the park for help. He had to determine whether what he saw was real or not. A soccer game was going on in the middle of a field. Hamilton dashed up to a man taking photos with his cell phone, grabbed his arm, and pleaded, "Do you want to take a picture of a big bird? It's as big as a penguin."

"No thanks, mister," replied the man. "My daughter is playing in the match."

Boink! A soccer ball had zoomed out of bounds and hit Hamilton in the head. He stuck out his hand to break the fall and regained his feet.

"Are you all right, mister?" asked the man.

Hamilton nodded.

The man turned him around and pushed him in the direction of a construction crew saying, "Maybe you better go that way."

Hamilton plodded toward a crew of men, garbed in yellow vests and white hard hats, that were digging a deeper channel in a V shape. He could see where it would eventually merge with the existing channel, which was shaped like a U. When he got near them, he yelled, "What are you doing? You're going to mess up the canal for the big bird. It looks like a penguin."

"There ain't no penguins around here," said an older man with a wrinkled face.

"Maybe he means the Orioles," said a younger fellow. "You got to go to Camden Yards in Baltimore to see them."

"No, I'm talking about right over there," said Hamilton. He turned around but had lost his orientation. He couldn't figure out what direction he had come. He thought about the bird losing its home because of the construction and screamed, "You're going to destroy his home... the penguin."

"Move on, bud. We got work to do."

Hamilton shuffled away, unsure of where he was going.

The older man told the younger one, "Jeb, this will get you ready for street work. You meet all types of drivers and they're always upset."

"But he's walking."

Hamilton staggered toward the street. He saw a line of children, maybe a half dozen in all, following their parents toward the Barbara Fritchie House. When he got near them, he yelled, "You kids want to see a big bird?"

The kids chanted, "Big Bird! Big Bird! Sesame Street!"

"No, he's right over here," said Hamilton, pointing toward the canal. Just then brakes screeched and a car veered into him, lifting him up onto its hood.

Tumbling off, he felt dazed.

"What are you doing?" yelled the driver, getting out of the car. "Are you all right?"

Hamilton got up, stomping his feet. "I think so."

The driver seemed incredulous, "You walked right into traffic without looking."

119

"Big bird is over there," said Hamilton.

"Here's a dollar," said the driver. "Stop wandering into the street."

Hamilton, changing directions once again, trudged toward a gazebo. A few men were sitting with their backs against its wall. When he got near them, he held onto the side of the structure to prop himself up and slurred, "Have you seen a big bird around here?"

"Gus, you got any T-bird," said one man to the other.

"Nope, just this ripple. Had a pint of T-bird sometime last week."

"You've seen the bird?" asked Hamilton again, leaning closer.

"We can give you some of this ripple." The man got up and held the end of the bottle near Hamilton's mouth.

He tried to push the man's hand away, but some of the wine spilled onto his shirt.

Hamilton turned once again and staggered deeper into the park. He saw an old lady with gray hair sitting at an easel near the woods. The sun was bearing down on him and his hips hurt from being hit by the car. He fell to his knees and crawled toward the woman, occasionally pointing toward the canal and grunting, "Big bird…big bird!"

"Hush," whispered the woman, who was brushing paint onto a canvas with sweeping strokes. She turned her head and said, "You almost made me lose the moment."

"Big bird," he gasped, pointing once again toward the canal.

"A big bird?" asked the woman.

He nodded.

"Can you show me?"

He nodded again.

The old lady, who had round hips and was top heavy like an exotic dancer, wrapped her arm around him and helped him to limp toward the canal.

After going a few yards, he flopped to the ground and sprawled out with exhaustion.

"Let's see if I can find something to perk you up." The woman rooted around in her art supplies bag and pulled out a mini whiskey bottle. She held it to his lips.

He took a sip and gagged.

She chugged the rest without wincing. "A stiff, hard one keeps me going for the whole day. Now get up on your feet."

They walked about 20 yards when Hamilton wheezed.

The old lady let go of him.

Hamilton plopped to the ground, gulping in air as though it was a precious commodity.

"I hope you're not breathing heavy because of me," she said. "My name is Scarlett."

He exhaled and said, "I'm Hamilton. My wife's at the salon."

"Just my luck," said Scarlett, bending down to help him up again. "Let's not dawdle."

They wandered over to the canal and started going downstream. Hamilton noticed gardens lining the canal full of pink roses with fragrant blooms or marigolds with pointed yellow petals. Butterflies fluttered about and bees buzzed nearby. Even though it was a splendid sight, it didn't seem right. He blurted, "No, it's the other way."

"Very well."

They turned around and plodded upstream. This section of the canal had less development. Hamilton observed clusters of water lilies with shiny green fronds floating on the surface and white oval petals sprouting above the waterline. "There!" he said, pointing to the big bird.

"Oh, my," gushed Scarlett. "He's special, isn't he? Let's be quiet."

She crouched down and he did the same. The water flowed down the canal in a spout, but the bird did not budge. They could hear the soccer game going on, cars being driven down the street, and the gurgling of the water hitting the pool in the bottom of the canal. Then the bird plucked a finger-sized fish with its beak from the pouring water. Hamilton hadn't seen anything in the water even though he was staring right at it.

"This is absolutely wonderful." Scarlett led him away from the canal. "Don't tell a soul."

"I won't," said Hamilton. "But what about that construction up there?"

"Let me see what I can do." Scarlett handed him her business card. Then she got his phone number.

Hamilton retraced his steps along the canal and hustled back to the beauty salon. When he saw his wife waiting for him underneath the burgundy awning, he groaned, "Honey, I'm sorry I'm late."

She took one look at him and asked, "Buster, what have you been up too?"

He looked down at his clothes and noticed his pants ripped at the knees, his shirt stained with grease from rolling off the car, and his shoes caked with mud. He gasped, "I've been walking around the park."

She leaned closer and took a whiff. "I know you've been drinking in the pub. Did an Irish lass dance on your lap?"

"It's nothing like that. The bird!" he screamed. "This lady painting a picture of the woods saw it. Really!"

She rolled her eyes and huffed, "Take me home."

As usual his wife didn't say a word on the drive home. Maybe he was making a mistake by taking her to the beauty salon. He was trying to be attentive to her activities, but to no avail. She still hadn't said a word when they entered their house. Then he remembered the lady's business card. "She gave me a card," he blurted, taking it out of his shirt pocket.

Ingrid grasped the card and read it: "Madam Scarlett du Pre. *Oil Painting & Hands-on Sculpture.*" She placed her hands on her hips and asked, "Did she pose nude for you or did you for her?"

"It's nothing like that. She's an old lady."

"What about the hands-on sculpture? Did she sculpt the rise and fall of man?"

"I haven't seen anything she's done."

"This may as well say mistress. You never get thrilled about me." Ingrid stormed into the bedroom and slammed the door. She cracked it open a minute later and thrust a pillow and blanket into his hands, saying, "Buster, you're sleeping on the sofa."

The icy chill remained for a week, his wife turning away from him and seeking comfort under a swath of blankets in the bedroom. Meanwhile Hamilton ate meals out of tin cans and pinched a sciatic nerve, which caused bouts of pain, sleeping on the sofa. When he saw his life coach, he had to reenact his adventure several times.

Erik looked at him cockeyed and asked, "Did you see the big bird before or after that soccer ball smacked you in the head?"

Nobody believed his version of events. Then on a Thursday afternoon he got a call at work from Scarlett, who wanted to meet him downtown.

Hamilton stopped home to pick up Ingrid. On the way downtown he stopped the car at a red light and peeked west toward the mountains. He saw the sunshine waning and what looked like ketchup poured on the horizon. He was a bit jittery, but tried not to show it.

"So you want me to meet Scarlett at a rendezvous?" asked his wife. "Buster, I'm not into threesomes."

"It's nothing like that," he said. "She gave me this address on E. Patrick Street and told me to meet her there at 7:00 p.m."

Driving downtown, he saw that the traffic had thinned out. He cruised along E. Patrick Street and saw the cement building.

"This is city hall," said Ingrid. "We're going to meet your mistress in the shadow of city hall?"

"No. She said to meet her inside."

Hamilton parked the car farther down the street, and they got out. He saw a few shoppers shuffling along the sidewalk and couples heading into restaurants. They tugged open the big door, rode the elevator up to the second floor, and walked down a hallway. They entered a meeting room where a bunch of people had gathered to talk about the city's budget.

Scarlett wore a yellow dress with a V neck, her un-holstered boobs jiggling underneath. The other ladies donned dresses with high necklines. All of them carried their easels and art supplies as though they had just come from a painting session.

In the back there was a suspicious person with ruffled brown hair, dressed in cargo pants and a beige shirt with pockets for clips of ammo, who appeared to be spying on the group. Hamilton couldn't tell whether it was a woman or man. He asked Scarlett, "Is that person with your group?"

Scarlett shook her head and replied, "I'm ready for that poacher. Nobody is going to turn our bird into a trophy."

The meeting started with the mayor, city comptroller, and council president seated in front. The mayor wore a white dress shirt and had hair that looked like it had been shined with brown shoe polish, which was offset by his gray sideburns. He went over the items in the agenda: changes in zoning for businesses, tax issues, a change in the school district's budget, and finally their item.

"We come to the last issue on our agenda: Public Works. Mr. Graves, please tell us about the projects your department is working on."

"Yes, mayor," replied the director. "We are replacing the bridge over the Monocacy River, repaving several streets on the east side of town, and deepening the channel in the Carroll Creek canal through Baker Park."

Suddenly, an uproar came from the old ladies in the room. "Mayor Davenport," said Scarlett, "may we have this panel's attention?"

"Why yes," said the mayor. "Please tell us your concerns."

"I represent the Frederick League of Landscape Painters. We have painted several portraits of an exquisite bird called a blue heron we would like to show you."

"Please do," stated the mayor.

The clerk lined up the eight paintings on easels as though it was an exhibition. The women represented a diverse spectrum of styles. One portrait showed the heron in such detail you could see wrinkles under its eyes and a double chin and another showed such depth and accuracy it would look good on a postage stamp. One painting was crafted in a geometric style - an orange triangle for the beak, gray rectangle for the body, and blue oval for the head. One piece was in the style of a Jackson Pollock painting with drips of colored pigments in swirls, letting the viewer decide whether to gaze in a clockwise or counterclockwise circle to take it all in. A plein-air watercolor was hazy throughout as though Monet had taken time out from painting lilies. An oil featured little dabs of paint for feathers and a brilliant blue sky reminiscent of Vincent van Gogh. The next painting was done in a scary surrealistic style with the bird flapping its wings for flight, causing a tornado to spin. And the last one was wholesome because it depicted a heron giving a hungry fledgling a fish to eat.

His wife whispered, "That is a big bird."

"As you can see, this magnificent heron has become a unique tourist attraction drawing painters from all over the area, photographers, and people who are just happy that Baker Park is pristine enough to provide habitat," stated Scarlett. "Therefore, we are asking the Public Works Department to refrain from taking any actions to damage that habitat."

"Mayor, I would like to say something to the board," said the person with the unisex look, who stood up in the aisle. "My name is Jan "Big Game Hunter" Wellington. I have travelled to Asia, Africa, and Alaska to hunt wild game. I believe that birds…."

Scarlett had taken a painting off an easel, tiptoed down the aisle, and raised the canvas high into the air. When she slammed it onto Jan's head, the painting ripped, pinning her arms to her body. Scarlett pushed the poacher into a corner seat and muttered, "You need a timeout."

Jan, still dazed, mumbled, "…should be on the dinner table or in cages."

Scarlett strutted to the front of the gallery and announced in a sweet voice, "Mayor, there are no objections."

"Very well," said the mayor, who appeared to be looking at her cleavage. He turned to the public works director and asked, "Mr. Graves, is it necessary to refurbish this canal?"

"Why no, Mayor Davenport. We were deepening the channel to aid in storm water runoff, but we can use manual labor to unclog any debris."

"Then it is the ruling of this panel that your department fill more potholes on a prompt basis."

"Yes, Mayor Davenport."

"This meeting is adjoined."

Scarlett turned to Hamilton and declared, "You are a hero."

All the ladies gathered around to thank him and took turns hugging him. They began to pack up their paintings.

"Scarlett, you seem to be a woman of many talents," said Ingrid. "Have you ever been a stripper?"

"It is a virtue to be modest," replied Scarlett. Then she winked at Hamilton and said, "Only my gentlemen friends know for sure."

His wife gave him the evil eye.

"I wasn't fooling around with her," said Hamilton. "Honest!"

"No?"

"Let's leave."

Hamilton and his wife took the elevator down to the lobby and went outside. Nighttime had descended and the street was silent. They scooted along the sidewalk looking for their car. Wings flapped in the air and some breed of bird streaked by.

"That's not a bat," said Hamilton, who drifted that way. "Let's see where it goes."

"Hold on, buster," said Ingrid, grabbing his arm. "Being a champion of one bird is enough."

Red Cloud

JEN AND NICK ALWAYS sat together in the back of Mr. Thatcher's American history class because he was an old geezer with gray hair who rattled on about things that happened a couple hundred years ago. Jen was country cool. Even though she grew up as a wildflower on a farm and was raised on wholesome foods like honey and alfalfa sprouts; she painted her fingernails, experimented with makeup, and played *Spin the Bottle* in grade school. She wore Daisy Dukes and downloaded singles by Keith Urban and Sugarland in Middle School. And now in high school she colored her hair with platinum-blonde highlights and dressed in petite blouses to tease the boys. On her first date with Nick she told him, "Any man of mine must treat me right." He opened doors, bought her a present, and took her to the local Double-T Diner for dinner and to the Leesburg Royal to see a movie. Afterwards, he acted like he didn't know what to do. She gazed up at him, batted her eyelashes, and purred, "Are you gonna kiss me or not?" He did. Nick was cool because he owned a car at the ripe age of 18. All the neighborhood kids gawked at his beat-up Volkswagen bug as though it was a spaceship that took him to places no one else had ever been to before. Even though his family was Calvinist and only allowed him to listen to classical music or bluegrass at home; he would drive down to the railroad tracks with Jen, park the car, and listen to DC 101, a rock station out of the nation's capital. Their shoulders were hunched over and their heads hanging down as they texted on their cell phones. Mr. Thatcher was pacing around the room and talking, "The Crown appointed John Campbell, 4th Earl of Loudoun, to be the Governor of Virginia…"

CTC (Care to talk?) Nick sent to Jen.

K (okay) ☺

RUB (Are you bored?)

LD (Like duh)

W2M@SS (Want to meet at the sub shop?)

"Hand them here!"

"Huh?" gasped Nick.

Mr. Thatcher was towering over them with a stern expression. "Your cell phones. You know it's against school policy."

They meekly handed over the devices.

Their teacher strode to the front of the room with his heels clacking on the floor in triumph and placed the cells on the corner of his desk where everyone could see them. "Now that we have the attention of Nicholas and Jennifer, let's proceed... Governor Campbell led several expeditions during the French and Indian War. The British and Iroquois fought against the French and Algonquian, though tribal loyalty was often in flux..."

Nick glanced at Jen and saw her violet eyes sparkle. He drifted on their sheen like a sailor adrift on an ocean in the twilight, not sure of where the current was taking his ship. He was still bobbing on the swelling waves that evening at the sub shop and the next morning in his living room at home. He stood at the bottom of the stairs, looked up, and hollered, "Mom, we're leaving now."

"Please take Todd with you or else," a high-pitched voice yodeled back.

"Okay."

"And thank Pastor Jones for leading the weekend retreat."

"I will."

The couple went out to the Volkswagen bug with his younger brother in tow. Nick opened the passenger door for Jen while his brother plopped behind the driver's seat. Nick scolded him, "Don't sit behind me. Sit over here."

"What's wrong with you?" whined Todd.

"That's where the car battery is...underneath the backseat. I don't want your fat butt squashing it."

Todd shimmied over behind Jen. She thought, *I can't believe we're going on a weekend camping trip with this 14-year-old brat.* She told her parents it was through Nick's church although he habitually skipped the Wednesday youth gatherings. Nick drove toward Tucker's Gap in a secluded part of Shenandoah Valley. She whined, "It's too bad we can't be alone."

"You heard my mom. We got to take him with us or else."

"Or else what?"

"Or else," he whispered, "she might find out we're going out here by ourselves."

"Oh, well." She turned to Todd, "We're glad you could join us."

Todd was munching on a Three Musketeers and playing a video game with funky electronic pings and music coming out of his earphones.

She turned around and fumed, "What a jerk!"

Nick turned off the main road and came to a junction with a gas station and convenience store. He pulled up to a pump, opened his knapsack, and ordered his brother, "Give me what you got."

"Huh?"

"Empty out your pockets. We're not buying nothing we don't need."

Todd reached into the front pocket of his dungaree jacket and pulled out a Kit-Kat bar, Reese's Peanut Butter cups from the side pockets, another Three Musketeer bar from his pants pocket, a quarter bag of Hersey's kisses from his back pants pocket, and a few Almond Joy bars from the other pants pocket.

Nick gave Jen a five and said, "Get what else we need."

She returned with a plastic bag that was squirreled away with Todd's munchies into Nick's knapsack. They pulled out of the gas station, drove on a gravel road for several miles, came to a dirt lot, and parked. Only one other vehicle was there - a black pickup with a gun rack in the cab. They got out their knapsacks from the Volkswagen's trunk and surveyed the wilderness.

A green bowl stretched for five miles in diameter and was surrounded by mountains. Two trails, one marked with yellow-blazes, led to the left and the other, a blue-blazed trail, led to the right. Either one would take them up to the rim and then they could follow that around on a two-day journey, but Todd burst out, "Let's go straight through."

129

"We can't do that," replied Nick. "There ain't nothing there but runoff and bogs. We'll never make it."

"We can bushwhack through the way the old pioneers did."

"They weren't that stupid. What happens if we can't make it by nightfall?"

"I got a couple hammocks from the GI surplus store."

Nick looked to Jen for guidance. Her face said *Nothing doing*.

Todd piped up, "I'll tell mom we didn't go with the church Crusaders."

Jen gritted her teeth and grinned, "We'd love to go tramping through the bog."

They slung knapsacks and hammocks over their shoulders and began hiking. The extra weight didn't bother Jen, who had done her share of chores around the farm from picking vegetables to mending fences. Nick glanced at a compass and guided them northwest, which would slice the valley in half. Water trickled in creeks that sprung up out of nowhere and the ground was soft and mushy. They came to a windswept plateau without any grass or bushes. Quartz glittered here and there in a rainbow of aquamarine, purple, and pink; and mica sparkled silver and gold. Todd ran in circles, kicked rocks with his boot, and scraped the soil with a penknife. He leaned over and picked up a lead ball, "Look at this rifle shot."

"That's from the pickup's gun," said Jen.

"It didn't come from there," countered Nick. "It's an old musket ball from centuries ago."

Todd leaned over again and picked up a splinter of rock, "Look at this arrowhead."

They all came together, leaned over, and inspected the arrowhead he held in his palm which was about two inches long and very thin, having been chipped down from a shard of gray flint. Nick was puzzled. "This must have been a battlefield, but what were they fighting over? There's nothing here."

Todd and Nick scooted around and turned over rocks and dug through the exposed soil with their boots and hands while Jen watched. She wasn't going to break any of her fingernails doing something so gross. The boys found three more musket balls and about a dozen arrowheads.

They hiked into a wood of sycamore and white oak. The air was heavy with humidity and the creeks became more numerous, fed by runoff from the mountains all around, and wisps of fog hung everywhere. Nick's boot slipped into the mud with a sucking sound, then he staggered away with a mush…mush… Trees thinned out and were replaced by thorny bushes and clumps of wildflowers here and there. They had only tramped two or three miles by late afternoon, but were tired. They spotted another rise up ahead and followed a deer path toward it. They dropped their gear at the base of a hill that was at least two stories tall and covered by brush and patches of black-eyed Susan and purple irises. They circled the mound until Jen stopped and gasped, "What's this?"

A stone staircase spiraled upward.

"Cool," said Todd. "Let's see where it goes."

As they climbed, lizards slithered out of their way. The top, which was as bare as a bald mountain, contained a stone foundation that outlined the shape of some type of structure.

"It's an abandoned house," said Nick.

Up here?" questioned Jen.

"Maybe it's a colonial fort," guessed Todd.

"You know what I think it can be," said Nick

"What?" asked Jen.

"Some type of religious shrine like Stonehenge or Machu Picchu."

"We're high enough, you know."

When they stood up, they peered into the crowns of shorter trees and saw many birds winging their way through the air, barely out of reach. A few put on a courtship display that consisted of pirouettes and loops and an assortment of chirps and whistles. The birds darted in and out of what may have been a doorway and pranced on a line of rocks that could have been a wall.

Todd raced around the stones yelling, "Where are the pigs? Where are the pigs?" scaring off the winged troubadours who flew to safety in nearby branches.

"The what?" asked Jen.

"He's talking about the Angry Birds game on his Droid," replied Nick. "He's always playing it."

"Oink!…oink!…" sounded Todd.

"Todd, come here!" commanded his brother. When he came over, Nick wrapped his arm around his shoulder, "There ain't no pigs out here. If any animals are stealing their eggs, it's probably snakes or raccoons."

"Are you sure?"

"I'm sure."

Jen was now inspecting the wall and doorway, "This could be somebody's party spot."

"I don't think so," said Nick. "Where are the empty beer cans and shattered wine bottles?"

"Like duh! Not now," she replied. "In the future."

"This would be a cool place to camp," said Nick.

"Yeah, let's do it."

They raced down the winding stone staircase to fetch their knapsacks. Then they humped up the path toward their secret hideaway. The stone structure was in sight when they heard the pounding of hooves and saw an Indian warrior riding an appaloosa pony, which kicked up dirt as it stopped in front of them, blocking the staircase. The Indian was half naked with his arms and chest layered with muscles and wearing buckskin briefs and moccasins. Coal-black eyes peered out of a ruddy face and his head was shaved except for a Mohawk of wild black hair. Squiggly scars that resembled the crest of a thunderstorm were carved on his cheeks. He held up a spear decorated with falcon feathers and spoke in an ominous voice, "I am Red Cloud, protector of this sacred ground."

"Ah!" screamed Todd, who hid behind his brother.

"Where did you come from?" asked Nick.

The Indian threatened, "Move on before you offend the Great Spirit."

"What are you talking about?" asked Jen. "There's nothing up there but a rundown building."

"Once a Shawnee village was nestled between the creek's fork. A fence surrounded it made of tree trunks sunk into the ground and thin branches woven like a basket. Hunting parties stopped on the bluff and saw fields of corn, carrots, potatoes, and squash tilled by their squaws. Children ran in and out of wigwams made of dried cattails. Over there stood a smokehouse with walls made from unfolded bark.

Behind me was the burial ground of the chiefs and shamans. Over the past thousand years when an elder passed into the other world, their house or temple would be razed, baskets of dirt would be carried over from the creek bank and dumped to cover up their possessions and a new house or temple would be built upon the old."

"Like, we didn't know or nothing!" yelped Todd.

"Let's find another spot to pitch camp," said Nick.

"Go around this place," warned Red Cloud. "Inland lives the creature with big foot."

"We can take care of ourselves," huffed Jen.

"Yeah, we know what we're doing," agreed Nick.

"If you go, beware."

As they trotted back down the path, they looked at each other in disbelief. They heard Red Cloud's feet stomp on the ground as he dismounted.

"Is he telling us the truth?" wondered Nick.

"It's got to be the truth," said Todd. "Why else would he be out here?"

"What difference does it make? It's not his property," griped Jen. "I didn't see a *No Trespassing* sign anywhere. We should go back and pitch camp where we want."

"I ain't messing with him," said Nick. "Not when he's got that spear in his hand."

"Me neither," agreed Todd.

"That's what I get for going camping with two slackers."

They walked into the woods talking among themselves. Jen said, "That wasn't a real Indian, you know. That was the man in the pickup."

"How could Red Cloud be him? He had a horse."

"He taught it to lay down in the back like a dog."

"I didn't see any blankets in the pickup. You ain't going to get a horse laying down on steel."

"What about hay to eat?" piped up Todd.

"Yeah?"

"Do I have to explain everything to you guys?" She couldn't believe what jug-heads men are.

133

They came to a small clearing and looked back toward the mound. Red Cloud was kneeling on top with arms spread, staring at the sky, and chanting, "Ihesdi niganayeguna ogiduda adanvdo (Keep safe our father's spirit)."

They plodded deeper into the bog, getting stuck on thorn bushes, and trudging through the mud which was too thin to plow and too thick to drink, which explained why this parcel of land had never been developed. Jen stepped on clumps of grass and scattered rocks to keep her Pedro Garcia platform boots and rhinestone jeans from getting nicked or soiled. They came to a place that had several large bushes to string hammocks from and decided to camp. While Nick gathered rocks to make a fire pit, Todd toyed with his Droid. He whined, "This ain't working right."

Nick took a look at the blank screen and said, "We got no reception out here. We got no nothing."

"We're in the land that time forgot," observed Jen.

Nick gathered twigs and started a fire. Jen looked up at the layer of clouds overhead which blotted out the starry sky and sighed. Her romantic getaway was anything but. Todd stood ankle deep in the mud near the fire and yelled, "Breakout!", and pantomimed the antics of a video game: juggling invisible balls that rocketed a thousand feet into the air and smashed into the cloud deck above. But no matter how many times he played, he couldn't bust a hole through to the stars. They were hemmed into this dark and dreary place.

When the fire was crackling and leaping a foot high, Nick opened his knapsack. He pulled out a bag of marshmallows and a box of graham crackers. Jen skewered the first marshmallow with a stick and toasted it over the orange flame until it turned golden brown. Then she melted a Hersey's kiss, which filled the air with a savory aroma as strong as a chocolate factory, and placed that on top the marshmallow and in-between two graham crackers. Nick did the same but burnt his marshmallow to a bubbly black. Todd melted a Reese's peanut butter cup in the fire and sandwiched the treat between graham crackers. Over and over again they roasted the marshmallows and melted chocolate and savored the S'mores. Afterward, Jen declared, "That's the best meal I ever had."

Nick boasted, "It's better than the best."

And Todd kept chewing on another S'more, his 15th by his own count.

Filled to the brim, they unrolled two hammocks and strung them between bushes. Jen climbed into one and gave Nick a longing look. The night air was biting and she wanted to cuddle with her boyfriend.

"I ain't sleeping by myself," complained Todd, who went over and began to climb into the hammock with her.

She pushed him out and screamed, "Get away from me…ew!"

So Jen spent the night hugging herself to keep from getting too cold. And Nick and Todd slept toe to head, making for a smelly night.

The next morning Todd was the first one up, rummaging through the camp. He pestered Nick, "Where's my Droid? Where's my Droid?"

"Why do you need your Droid? We ain't going nowhere."

"Maybe I can get it working again. I want to play Dragon Warrior with my friend in Tokyo."

"In my knapsack."

"Where's your knapsack?"

"Underneath the hammock, stupid."

"Where?"

Nick turned to look. His knapsack wasn't there or anywhere else in sight. He went over to the other hammock. Jen was sound asleep with a grin on her face as though she was dreaming about something pleasant, using her knapsack as a pillow. He shook her and yelped, "Wake up! Wake up!"

"Unh! Is it morning?" A bit of sunlight was filtering through the clouds which were beginning to break up.

"Do you know where my knapsack is?"

"Like duh! How would I know where you put it? I've been sleeping."

Nick searched under both hammocks and around the smoldering ashes of the campfire and in nearby bushes.

"Hoof prints," hollered Todd.

Nick hurried over and saw a line of hoof prints leading over a small knoll. "They're too big to be a deer."

"It's Red Cloud's horse," huffed Jen. "Indians don't shoe their horses like us."

"I'm not going after him," said Nick. "Not with that spear."

"He's got our food," whined Jen.

"And my Droid," added Todd.

"And my compass," admitted Nick.

They followed the tracks to a wood of weeping willows four to six stories tall with vines wrapped around the trunks and bushes sprouted up in the crevices of branches where the soil had clumped together around wind-blown seeds. The ground was pockmarked by puddles turned black from rain percolating through the roots. Underneath the canopy it was so dark they could barely see. They crept along carefully to avoid sinking into the pools or stepping on snakes. The tracks stopped. Leaves crinkled above. Todd looked up and stammered, "Do you see them?"

Branches seemed to be moving, expanding and contracting, and hidden behind the shaggy foliage, moving in slow-motion, were creatures dangling upside down with dark brown fur except for their shoulders and heads which were snow-white. Lodged in-between intertwined vines, several stories up, was Nick's bright blue knapsack. If he could somehow climb up the branches to reach those vines and yank them apart, the knapsack might fall loose. But the sloths in a zoo were only two or three feet long. These behemoths were easily 12 to 15 feet in length, bigger than orangutans or gorillas. They could probably crush his ribs or strangle him, if he was foolish enough to get too close and wrestle with one. A thud sounded nearby. A sloth had flopped down that was twice his size, appearing out of nowhere like a Halloween ghost.

"Aaaahhhh!" he yelled as he bounded away faster than a white-tail deer in flight.

Jen and Todd fell in behind him, sliding in the wet soil and splashing through puddles.

At the campsite they gasped for breath and tripped over each other packing up their gear. They wandered about in the bog, dazed and disoriented, afraid to enter the woods for fear of running into more giant sloths. They crisscrossed their path, sometimes curling back around, suffering from the sweltering heat and swarms of gnats and flies that popped up out of nowhere to bit their arms and faces. Jen stomped through the mud unladylike, cussing and shaking her head, Nick shivered with fright, and Todd kept babbling about searching for the philosopher's stone in the World of Warcraft. They had wandered about for hours when they heard wild whooping and saw the appaloosa pony charging toward them with Red Cloud hunched forward. The horse reared up and whinnied and a spear whistled through the air and landed right in front of Nick's feet. The Indian swung the horse back around and dismounted and came face to face with him. Up close Jen could see his stocky build and a necklace of bear claws. Her boyfriend was a string bean compared to that ripe tomato. Red Cloud spoke, "You turn and go."

Nick was petrified, "We're going. Which way? Yes, that way."

"You could at least help us get home," she screamed. "A sloth that lives in your forest took our knapsack and now we're lost."

Red Cloud mumbled, "Squaw belongs in wigwam with papoose..."

"What'd you say?"

He strutted over and sneered, "Squaw belongs in wigwam with papoose sucking her breast." He turned his cheek, daring her to slap him.

With the rage built up inside of her from sleeping in a cold hammock all night long by herself, from not spending one minute alone with her boyfriend because of his bratty brother, from not eating anything for breakfast or lunch, from getting mud splashed on her new pair of boots and rhinestone jeans, and from having this man talk down to her as though she was a child, she curled her fingers into a fist. Then she leaned back and flung a right hook so swift and hard it landed with the wallop of a prizefighter...smack!

Red Cloud went flying through the air, completely suspended off the ground for a second or two, and landed in the mud with a solid flop, squirting slim everywhere. He cried out, "Waya adanvdo ehi hawiditlv agiya (Wolf spirit lives in woman)."

"Jen, what have you done?" asked Nick.

"That was worth breaking two fingernails," she bragged.

The Indian shook his head, gathered himself, and stood up to face them. He grabbed a stone tomahawk hooked to his buckskin brief.

Nick trembled and begged, "She didn't mean to do it. We're sorry, Mr. Red Cloud, we really are. Please don't get mad."

He was silent for a moment before he spoke, "Woman, I take you to mountain trail."

Red Cloud put Jen on his pony and hustled out in front to lead them.

"How do you stay on this thing?" she wondered. There was no saddle to sit on or reins to hold. She dug her heels into the pony's ribs, centered her weight on its back, and grabbed its mane. The pony moved with a smooth gait, making her feel as though she was floating on a cloud, while Nick and Todd stumbled in the mud behind her, dodging horse apples.

They passed by the burial mound in the twilight. A harsh cackle, kleek-ik-ik, sounded above. The building on top looked luminous in the fading light like a gateway to the heavens. Red Cloud led them to a trail that went up to the rim of the mountain. Jen dismounted, and they hiked upward. He chanted, "Asgotanv dikata wohali adasehede nehi (Let eyes of eagle guide you)."

The sun had set, but its reflection off the moon provided ample light. They scooted around huge boulders, the smallest being as big as tombstones, and hiked maybe a mile until they got back to the dirt parking lot. "Hey, look," screamed Nick, "The pickup is still here. Maybe that fellow is going hunting overnight again."

"Maybe it's stolen," gushed Todd as he pantomimed throttling a joystick, "Grand Theft Auto…zoom…watch out…errrrrr…"

"You know who it is," said Jen, gazing back toward the trail.

They climbed into the Volkswagen bug. Todd's stomach growled from the backseat. "I'm hungry too," admitted Jen. Nick drove back to the gas station and convenience store. As soon as they rambled inside, Jen made a beeline to bakery goods and Todd to the refrigerated section. She came back with a Ho Hos cream-filled chocolate cake and Todd dug into a quart of Ben & Jerry's Triple Caramel Chunk ice cream. Nick picked up a bag of Utz potato chips and a Pepsi and went toward the counter. An elderly man with thinning white hair and bifocals had plopped behind the cash register. Nick muttered, "Wait until we tell him about Big Foot."

They saw a painting of an Indian warrior on the wall: proud, bordering on arrogant, with three falcon feathers sticking up from the back of a Mohawk and scarlet semi-circular scars on his cheeks.

"That's Red Cloud!" screeched Jen.

"Yeah," agreed Nick, "that's a portrait of Red Cloud."

The store owner chuckled, "Everybody, in these here parts, knows about Red Cloud. Shawnee warrior. Died in the 1758 uprising."

"In 1758?"

"He was the fiercest fighter of his tribe. Perhaps the smartest. He almost united the entire Shawnee nation."

They paid for their stuff and walked out.

"If he died in 1758," asked Nick, "then who did we see?"

"He could have been a great-great-grandson," said Jen. "You know, the name and tradition passing from one generation to the next."

"Or maybe not," said Todd.

Nick sighed. "Our Big Foot sighting is nothing compared to him."

They turned onto the highway where the headlights of other cars glowed brighter than the white sphere above. A groan came from the backseat. Todd's eyes were darting all over the place, unable to focus on anything. He began ranting, "Where's my Donkey Kong, my Gotham Racing, my Super Mario…"

Todd went into a spasm with his whole body shaking, pain shooting through his arms and chest, and perspiration beading up on his brow. He looked like a hospital patient going into cardiac arrest, Code Blue.

Nick and Jen were finding out what a lot of campers already knew: a few days in the wilderness can lead to video game withdrawal. She leaned over the front seat and put her hand on Todd's shoulder, "Calm down." She looked at Nick.

"I'm driving as fast as I can."

"We got to get him connected to the net."

Todd was ranting again, "Where's my Xbox, my Nintendo 64, my Star Wars - Battlefront, my Street Fighter, my Madden NFL…"

Nick drove to Jen's farm. They got out and moseyed up the gravel driveway. He turned to face her. In the moonlight her violet eyes gleamed like gems, translucent and hypnotic, drawing him in. Her kiss was as soft as the clouds and as moist as the bog. She said, "I wish you could stay longer."

"You know I got to take my brother home."

"I know."

In that moment he realized what could have been on this fragile night underneath the glittering stars.

When he got back to the car, Todd was squirming in the backseat, mumbling to himself, lost in the deep throes of withdrawal. Nick drove as fast as he could the last two miles home. He helped his brother get out. Todd was hunched over, gasping for breath. Nick sat him down at his computer console and flipped on the power. Zap...the screen came to life. Todd's breathing returned to normal and his hands stopped shaking. Nick quipped, "Thank God for 4G."

It was after midnight. Nick spent at least an hour cleaning his boots before he settled into bed. He probably got less than five hours sleep. The next morning he found himself in the American history class lounging in the back row with Jen, whose eyes were so droopy she could have been mistaken for one of Snow White's seven dwarfs, Sleepy. He tried to listen to Mr. Thatcher's lecture, but soon faded out. Screech...the metallic scraping of a trash can and its reverberating ring filled his ears. Mr. Thatcher had kicked the can across the front of the room, waking up half the class. The old teacher was still babbling, "There were skirmishes all across the Shenandoah Valley with the tribes of the Algonquian Nation. Some would call them battles...." Nick wondered if he had just imagined the burial mound and Red Cloud. Was it only a daydream? He searched his pockets, but couldn't find his cell. He sat straight up and leaned forward as far as he could, trying to see the top of Mr. Thatcher's desk. Their cells were not there. Did he drop it in the bog? He wasn't sure what was going on. He peered at his hand and spread his fingers. It looked as if soil and specks of quartz were stuck underneath his nails.

Mission Control to Thomas Hardy

THE BUDGET BATTLES THAT raged in Congress spilled into the streets. Protesters, hungry and haggard from marching all day, lunged and leered at the employees leaving the Supersonic Spacecraft Company. Thomas Hardy leaned toward a woman parading toward her car in the parking lot and screamed, "We're going to shut your company down!"

Her black hair was pulled behind her ears and her eyes stayed focused on something in the distance. She peered straight ahead through her dark-rimmed glasses, paying no mind to the protestor who stood only three feet away.

Thomas, who had disheveled brown hair and a walrus mustache, pressed his mug closer and screeched again, "Don't want to talk to us, lady?"

She stepped into the parking lot and was shielded by a phalanx of security guards.

Thomas grunted his disdain.

A shorter woman, with round hips and a round face, pressed up against the fence. Even though it was only four feet high and could easily be jumped by a protestor, she blurted, "Athena doesn't have to say hello to you. You're trying to get rid of her job."

A thin, wiry woman who had been marching with Thomas all day, griped, "You might have spunk, lady, but you're just as bad as her. You're hiding behind a wasteful company that is squandering our taxes."

The woman placed both hands on her hips and wailed, "My name is Nora. I don't hide behind anybody. Take me on! I'd love to bust your lip open."

The woman protestor stepped back from the fence. Even though her brown hair was streaked with gray and her blue eyes had seen it all, her face registered shock.

Nora wagged her hips in triumph as she sashayed toward her car in the parking lot. She was swallowed up by the security detail.

A man in a white shirt and tan trousers, whose large belly hung over his belt and balding dome gleamed in the sunlight, stopped by the protestors. "My name is Brandon," he said. "I'm a supervisor in the gyroscope department. Maybe you don't understand what the space program is all about."

"We understand what we need to know," sneered Thomas. "We got roads with potholes and crumbling bridges. We want our tax money spent on those things."

Brandon pulled out his smart phone and tilted the display toward the man and woman. He stated, "I would like to show you and your wife what space exploration is all about."

"How do you know I'm married to him?" lashed out the woman as though her personal space had been violated.

"I looked out the window earlier today and saw you two together. It is obvious. Now let me show you this." He brought up a photo of a blue and white orb. 'This is a snapshot of the earth taken from the space station." Then he conjured an image of a colorful nebula. "And this is a photo taken by the Hubble Telescope."

"We don't need that junk," shouted Thomas. "We live off the grid."

"Yeah," agreed his wife. "We're living off the grid."

"Please yourself," said the man, pocketing his smart phone. He began to walk away.

Thomas screamed again, "We're going to shut your company down."

On the way home his wife knitted a cap, the needles clacking against each other, while he drove their jeep. Neither one said a word. For Thomas the mental picture of Athena, the stone-faced woman who passed by them during the protest, became the image of the Supersonic Spacecraft Company. She would rather spend her time inputting mathematical equations into a computer than acting like a human being. For his wife it was Brandon, the supervisor with the smartphone. She equated all electronic gadgets with dehumanization. She often saw teenagers who would rather text each other on those phones than talk. For her, the farmer's almanac was the most prized possession. Good since the time of Ben Franklin, it gave her baking recipes to try, wise sayings to think about, and a weather report for the entire year. Thomas pulled in front of their cabin on the outskirts of a hamlet just south of the Mason-Dixon Line. He strolled into the kitchen while his wife sat on the living room sofa to resume her knitting.

Thomas Hardy and his wife, Emma, enjoyed the simple pleasures. Thomas chipped firewood into pellets to fuel their stove, which heated their tiny home, hunted and trapped wild game, and cooked most of their meals in a rustic style. His wife crafted their clothes from fabric purchased from an Amish peddler and preserved jams made from peaches, cherries, grapes, apples, and apricots. She spent a lot of her time tending plants in their garden. Both of them became angry when they discovered that the Supersonic Spacecraft Company was involved in a bribery-kickback scheme that chiseled taxpayers out of their hard earned money. Thomas often worked construction jobs and Emma sewed quilts and made candles to sell at the farmer's market. They didn't want one penny of their taxes going to this scandal or to space exploration. They were not connected to cable, but learned of the whole affair from the *Potato Reaper*, a newsletter distributed among back-to-nature buffs like themselves. Conservatives claimed the newsletter was a socialist rag while liberals considered it fodder funded by corporations that had infiltrated their community. However, most of the contributors were plain people stating their opinions on different political and social issues. The couple never watched television, but that didn't mean they couldn't have fun. Thomas played a banjo and Emma plucked a fiddle. They hung out at Tucker's Inn on Friday evenings and sat in on bluegrass sessions with other musicians. Moses, an African-American man from Mississippi, blew a wicked harmonica and Randall, a drummer from Chicago, integrated jazz rhythms into their songs. At times they got all the customers stomping their feet, clapping, and spouting enough *Amens* and *Oh, Lords* to fill a church. And both of them were keen on reading the bible which contained no passages about rockets or spacecraft. The heavens were reserved for God's angels.

A banging sound came from the back door and then the hinges creaked. A middle-aged woman, whose weight had settled in her hips, stomped into the kitchen and said, "I was hoping to find you here."

"Sylvia, what's up?" asked Thomas.

"We want to thank you for leading the protest today," she said, straddling a chair. She had curly hair, no makeup covering the blemishes on her face, and owlish eyes. "We're going down to the D.C. suburbs this weekend. Bev and I will hand out leaflets at the shopping center. Ken and Jeff are going door-to-door in the neighborhood. We'll give the Supersonic Spacecraft Company a Columbus Day surprise they'll never forget."

"That's cool," said Thomas. "We should be back late Sunday evening so count us in. Do you think a lot of people will show up at the protest on Monday?"

"At least 500," stated Sylvia. "Definitely more than the criminal justice march. We'll make so much noise our chants will shake the windows and rock the foundation of their building. They'll think an earthquake is happening."

"I can't wait," gushed Emma. "Would you like a cup of tea?"

"Jeff's waiting in the car," she snapped. "I hope your camping trip is a blast."

"It will be," said Thomas. "We enjoy camping in the mountains."

"We'll see you." Sylvia slipped out the back door, which was always unlocked.

Thomas stepped onto the back porch and watched their car squeal down the street. He gazed into the northeastern sky. He spotted a couple cumulus clouds, but nothing threatening. If the horizon was purple that meant a cold front was blowing in. If it was yellowish, a warm front. It looked like nothing would mess up their trip. Even so he came back inside and asked Emma, "What does the almanac say about the weather?"

His wife scooted over to the coffee table and thumbed through it. When she reached a page in the back, she scanned down a list of dates. She announced, "60s during the day and low 40s at night."

"Cool, I can't wait," said Thomas.

They packed the jeep with their gear and hit the road Saturday morning. Thomas drove through Harper's Ferry toward the mountains in West Virginia. He followed country roads that paralleled the border with Virginia, climbing up hillsides, dipping down, rising again, and curving around mountains along treacherous cliffs. His wife chatted about the pattern she was quilting into a blanket and bemoaned the tax money squandered by the Supersonic Spacecraft Company. She fumed, "I can't believe that guy Brandon said we needed the space program."

"He didn't know what the heck he was talking about," grumbled Thomas. "We're going to spend billions of dollars for a bunch of photos?"

His wife simmered down and didn't respond. That settled it. Thomas was glad they were heading on this camping trip and could get away from the turmoil for a while. By the time he and his wife got back they would be refreshed and ready to go to the protest to raise Cain.

They cruised into the George Washington National Forest, pulled over to the roadside, and munched on fruit packed by his wife. Thomas started the jeep and headed farther into the forest. He drove on a gravel road and then an unmarked fire road up a mountainside. He parked by a grove of old-growth red oaks, which had wrinkled grayish-brown bark and green lichen surrounding their base, that had never been logged. It would take a chain of four or five people to encircle each trunk. The branches didn't begin until the trees reached a height of three stories, and he and his wife couldn't see the top of their crowns. They hiked down the trail, taking in the scent of the giant trees and crunching the acorns and pointed-brown leaves that had fallen with their boots.

They came to a clearing where a ring of stones had been charred by numerous campfires. They filled up their canteens at a nearby spring, but kept going. The trail rose over a ridge and went down a slope. Then it split in two, going north and south along a river. Hemlock trees hugged the banks with their evergreen tresses hanging over the water. They followed the southern trail and found a huge red oak to camp under. They ate sandwiches they had brought with them and put up their tent. They snuggled in their sleeping bags and listened to water trickling over rocks. The sound was so soothing they soon fell asleep.

Thomas was woken by his wife's shrieking. He jumped out of his sleeping bag, his teeth chattering with cold, and bumped into something solid. Ice pelted his face. He searched the floor for his backpack. Everywhere he crawled something crunched underneath him. He found it and flipped on his flashlight. A red oak branch had fallen on their tent, ripping it apart and scattering shards of bark everywhere. The top of the branch was covered with a half foot of snow. Ice pellets poured inside. His wife's face twisted in anguish as she screamed. He straddled her and pushed the branch, which was larger than any tree growing in their hamlet. It wouldn't budge. He got on all fours and pressed his back against it, lifting with his thighs and shoulders. He nudged the branch a bit, lessening the pressure on his wife, but she was still pinned. He fumbled through her backpack. He gave her a couple aspirins to dull the pain and let her drink as much water as she could. He covered her bare chest with his jacket, put a knit cap on her head, and slipped a pair of socks over her hands to keep her from getting frostbite. He kneeled beside her and said, "I'll get help."

She peered up at him and pleaded, "I don't want to die."

He stroked her chin. Realizing this might be the last time he saw her alive, he gazed into her blue eyes and purred, "I love you."

She kept repeating "I don't want to die" as if it were her mantra.

Thomas clambered over the branch and out of the tent. He pulled the torn flap shut as best he could and trudged up the trail with snow swirling all about. By the time he hiked half a mile, his shirt and pants were draped with icicles. The closer he got to their jeep, the faster he tramped. When he saw the hood, he dashed forward, splashing up snow and mud.

Thomas plopped into the driver's seat and slammed the door shut. He rubbed his hands together to warm them and jangled the keys. He inserted the key into the ignition and started the jeep. Thomas pumped the gas pedal with his foot, but the engine conked out. He turned the ignition again and pressed down on the gas. Once again the motor started and stopped. He had flooded the engine. He counted his breaths as he waited for the gas to recede…one…two…

three…all the way to 10. He turned the key again. The battery grinded, but the jeep would not start. He waited another moment and cranked the ignition again. The battery grinded, then went out. Snow swirled all around the jeep. He beat the dashboard with his fist and yelped, "Damn!"

He had to get out and hike to the ranger station even though it was a dozen miles away. Time was critical. He didn't know how long his wife could survive pinned underneath that red oak branch. Why hadn't they camped in the clearing? Why didn't they realize that a storm was coming? He had read the signs in the sky on Friday evening, but the front swept in from a different direction and pulled down frigid air from the arctic. As he trudged through the snow, his body shook with convulsions. Hypothermia was creeping upon him.

Thomas had hiked 10 to 15 miles on trails many times before. He stumbled and grabbed onto a tree trunk to keep from falling into the snow. His boots and pants were caked with snow, ice, and mud. Each foot landed with a dull thud. He tripped and flew forward. He put out his hands to break the fall and plopped into the snow. He got up to his knees and tried to stand. Every time he took a step, he fell again, limping along the ground like a bird with a broken wing.

Thomas dropped to the ground, unable to get up. He crawled along the sunken path on his knees and elbows like a baby. Still he willed his way forward. He lunged headfirst into the snow, tremors shaking his whole body. Oh, God, he thought, unable to complete the sentence. He wiggled like a worm, sliding through the snow and mud. Then he stopped.

Wind whistled through treetops and pushed the clouds north. A half-moon and cluster of stars appeared above. The celestial orbs shined down on the crumbled body lying in the snow. Flurries still swirled about, covering everything, including him, with an icy white layer.

Rhythmic crunching came closer and closer. A pair of hikers plodded down the trail in snowshoes. The lead hiker, who swung his flashlight back and forth, gasped. The man, who had a park service badge on his coat, plopped down on all fours and rolled Thomas over.

Ice and mud was caked on his face. His breathing was barely audible.

The park ranger shouted, "Jake, get over here. He's still alive!" Both of them kneeled overtop him.

Thomas tried to speak, but could not mutter a sound.

The hikers propped him up and pulled his shirt and pants off. Jake unraveled what looked like a roll of tin foil.

Thomas tried to resist, but every muscle in his body was drained and becoming stiff from the cold.

They slipped his legs into an aluminum sheath and wiggled it over his stomach and chest. They propped his head up on a knapsack and sheltered him from the wind by pulling over a log. The park ranger poured water from his canteen into a pouch and shook the mixture up and down. He kneeled down again and said, "Drink this."

Thomas gulped the drink down. It felt hot and tasted sweet. He could feel his throat loosening and stomach retaining heat. He mouthed the words, "Thank you."

"Don't thank us," chortled Jake. "Thank NASA. The space blanket and freeze-dried energy drink are courtesy of them."

Thomas thought this was all a dream. Was he still asleep? He still couldn't move his arms and legs.

"Are you out here alone?" asked the park ranger.

This time a sound came forth from his lips, "Wi... Wi...."

"Your wife is with you?" asked the park ranger, who was peering down at him. "If your wife is out here, blink your eyes."

Thomas blinked.

"What trail is she on?" he asked.

Thomas couldn't pronounce any words. He could only grunt a single sound, "Riv... Riv..."

"She's on the river?" asked the park ranger. "Blink your eyes."

Thomas blinked again.

"We're going to go after her," he said. "You'll be okay here."

Thomas nodded.

The park ranger turned to the other man and said, "Jake, we'll have to split up when we get down to the river. If you find his wife, shoot your flare."

"Let's go!" said Jake.

The hikers trotted through the snow, kicking up clumps with each step. When they wound down the hill, their snowshoes crunched the ice. The sound of the wind whistling through tree branches remained.

They had left, but Thomas Hardy saw something come into view before him. A supernatural spirit? The stone face of Athena took shape. He peered into her dark eyes and entered a passageway that led to her core. What was inside her mind was beyond his comprehension - strings of numbers and calculations based on algebra, calculus, and higher mathematical models. Thousands of equations described the arc of satellites, thrust of rockets, shapes of spheres, speed of sound and light, composition of matter and energy, internal construction of atoms, and even the meaning of time. Thomas could touch the petal of a flower and sniff its perfume, but not understand its composition. He could feel the warmth of sunshine or hear the tweeting of birds, but not fathom how. Even though everything inside Athena's mind was cold, it could bring forth an understanding of life. He snapped to his senses and gazed into the sky above. Stars burst forth.

He spotted the Big Dipper, and recalled his first camping trip as a boy. His father showed him the star pattern and how two stars aligned to point to Polaris, the North Star. "Follow that at night," said his dad, "if you want to go north."

Next Thomas traced the other stars which formed the handle and cup of the Little Dipper. Gazing south through a gap in the trees along the trail, he recognized the star pattern of Pegasus, the winged horse. How he wished he could ride that constellation to a safer place. Beyond these constellations were so many stars, with none of them being bright enough to stand out on their own, jumbled together to resemble white gauze, that were part of the Milky Way strewn across the night sky. He wondered how many solar systems and planets like earth were out there in distant space, millions of years away. He knew that some stars had burned out eons ago and were no more. Nonetheless, their light shined above.

Thomas saw an image of a satellite floating in an arc above the earth. Its wings were covered with photovoltaic cells that gathered unlimited power from the sun. He thought about the earth being a satellite that revolved around that star. Why couldn't mankind get all its energy from clean, renewable resources? The technology was available. Why pollute the air and water that people breathe and drink? He thought about the other inventions that NASA relied on to make space travel a possibility. The space station made and recycled all its water. Wastewater from respiration, sweat, and urine were turned into drinkable water. Why couldn't mankind recycle its water and other commodities such as wood, plastic, and aluminum? How many rainforests would be clear-cut and how many open-pit mines dug? Lastly, he thought about the hydroponic gardens that space colonies would cultivate. Such a Garden of Eden, with its drip irrigation, could out produce a farm field by 10 to 1. Did every wetland have to be drained and fallow land plowed for agriculture? Earth, the satellite, could go on for a long time without the wanton destruction of its natural resources. Wasn't that a message the space program was sending us?

He felt so frail lying there in an aluminum cocoon. His own body heat started to warm him up, causing him to come further into his wits. The ominous face of Athena appeared before him again - her long nose, dark eyes, and black hair pulled behind her ears - but she had no expression. He wondered why wisdom wasn't kind. Her lips had no mirth, the folds around her eyes were not crinkled, and her countenance grim. Then he realized that wisdom was what you made of it. Ignore it at your own peril. The mistakes he had made the day before - scanning the sky instead of relying on weather radar, camping underneath the boughs of an aged tree, and carrying lightweight, summer gear - flashed across his mind. He wanted to cry, but was filled with worry for his wife. Then he felt sorrow for the world. He did not know how long he had been lying there, whether for a few moments or an hour. The wind still whistled through tree branches and the night air stayed frigid.

There was a whoosh, and a blaze of red appeared in the sky. It was similar to the flame from a booster rocket lifting a capsule or satellite into orbit. Thomas could see a thousand rockets lifting off from earth sending the last remnants of the human species out into space. Some people would colonize distant planets; others would live their entire lives on space stations. It was destined to happen because of an unforeseen accident or mistake - a nuclear war, the supernova of the sun, a comet striking the planet, or climate change.

Made in the USA
Middletown, DE
30 May 2021